GOOSEBUMPS®

Also available as ebooks

ALSO AVAILABLE:

SAY CHEESE—AND DIE SCREAMING!

R.L. STINE

SCHOLASTIC INC.
New York Toronto London Auckland
Sydney Mexico City New Delhi Hong Kong

ISBN 978-0-439-91876-3

Goosebumps book series created by Parachute Press, Inc.

Goosebumps HorrorLand #8: *Say Cheese—and Die Screaming!* copyright © 2009 by Scholastic Inc.

21   18 19 20/0

Printed in the U.S.A.
First printing, March 2009

3 RIDES IN 1!

SAY CHEESE—AND DIE SCREAMING!

1

"Julie — wait up!" My best friend, Reena Jacobs, ran across the school hallway toward me. Her blond ponytail bobbed behind her. "Is that a new camera?"

I shook my head. "It's one of my old cameras." It swung from a strap around my neck. "Dad says he'll buy me a new one if I get the big assignment from Mr. Webb."

Reena blinked her green eyes. "Big assignment?"

I gave her a shove. "Reena, I've only been talking about it for *months*. Remember? To shoot the entire student body for the big two-page spread in the *Tiger*?" That's the name of our yearbook.

Reena scrunched up her face. "I thought Mr. Webb already chose David Blank for that."

"Well, you thought wrong," I said. "That's why I'm hurrying to the *Tiger* office. I've got an *awesome*

3

idea. No way Mr. Webb can say no to it. David can sit on his butt and watch *me* take the photo!"

Reena laughed. "You don't *like* David — do you?"

I rolled my eyes. "Does a lettuce like a goat?"

She frowned at me. "Goat? I don't get that, Julie."

With her light blond hair and big green eyes, Reena is very pretty. I think she's the prettiest girl at Twin Forks Middle School. And she's smart, too.

But she only understands straight talk.

"I meant David tries to gobble up everything," I explained. "He wants to be the only star. Mr. Webb asked *me* to shoot the bake sale in the gym last week. And when I showed up, guess who was there."

"David?"

"You got it," I said.

"He's very competitive," Reena said. Then she grinned. "But I think he's kind of cute."

"Cute?" I stuck my finger down my throat. "With that bright orange hair and those orange freckles? He looks like a *carrot*!"

"You have vegetables on the brain," Reena said.

"No, I've got *pictures* on the brain," I said. "I can be just as competitive as David. I really want to take that big photo. That's why I want to get to the yearbook office before David does."

I turned and started to jog down the hall. It was nearly three-thirty, and the school had emptied out.

"Julie —" Reena called after me. "Are we still going bike riding on Saturday?"

"I've got to watch Sammy in the morning," I said. Sammy is my little brother. "We can ride all afternoon."

I turned the corner and bumped right into the Sneer Sisters.

Actually, Becka and Greta aren't sisters. They're best best friends. I've never seen them apart.

I call them the Sneer Sisters because they both always sneer when they see me. Like I smell like rotten meat or something. And they're always so totally mean to me.

They even look a little alike. They are both tall and very skinny, and they both have long noses and kind of pointy chins. Like witch chins.

"Hi, Ju-Ju," Becka said, sneering.

I gritted my teeth. She knows I *hate* to be called Ju-Ju. That's what I called myself when I was too little to say the name Julie.

Greta pointed at my mouth. "Ju-Ju, you have something on your front teeth," she said.

I rubbed my teeth with my pointer finger. "Is it gone?" I asked her.

Greta nodded. "Yeah. It was your finger!"

They both slapped high fives and cackled like that was the funniest joke in history.

"Where did you get that joke?" I said. "First grade or second?" I pushed past them and hurried down the hall. My camera bounced in front of me as I jogged.

The yearbook office was the last door on the left. I grabbed the knob, twisted it, and burst inside.

And then I gasped as I was *blinded* by an explosion of white.

Okay. It wasn't an explosion.

A few seconds later, I started to see again. And David Blank slowly came into focus.

He was standing next to Mr. Webb. He had his camera raised. And a big grin on his carroty face.

"That's a lesson for you, Julie," he said. "That's how you take someone by surprise. An *awesome* candid shot."

"David — you nearly *blinded* me!" I cried. I still had white flashes in my eyes.

David stared at the view screen on the back of his camera. "The look on your face!" he cried. He shared it with Mr. Webb. "Like something in a horror movie."

"*You're* a horror movie!" I shot back angrily.

I was so disappointed that David was there. I elbowed him out of the way and tried to squeeze next to Mr. Webb. "You're leaving — right?" I said to David.

He shrugged. "I'm just hanging out," he said. "Mr. Webb and I were talking about some yearbook ideas."

Mr. Webb took off his glasses and rubbed his eyes. He is very tall and lanky. He's so skinny, the bones stick out of his wrists. He has a very narrow face, and his black hair is cut very short.

Some kids have a nickname for him. They call him The Needle because he really does look like one.

He has a soft voice. He always seems to stop and think for a long time before he answers a question. And he's always taking off his glasses and putting them back on. A nervous habit, I guess.

I've never had him as a teacher. But I think he's a good yearbook adviser. He's very fair. And he's always ready to listen to new ideas.

"My dad got me a new lens for my Pentax," David said. "I've got ten-times zoom on this camera. And twenty-times zoom on my other camera."

"Don't brag or anything," I said.

He thinks he's way cool because his dad is manager of Camera World, the camera store at the mall.

Mr. Webb pushed his glasses up on his nose and turned to me. "Julie, you got some nice shots of the wrestling team last week," he said. Then he added, "So did David."

I bit my lip. "I thought the wrestling team was *my* assignment," I said.

David grinned. "Just thought I'd back you up," he said. "You know. In case that little camera of yours broke or something."

Couldn't you *clobber* that kid?

"You said you have an idea you want to show me?" Mr. Webb asked.

I reached into my backpack and pulled out the plans I had drawn. If only David would disappear in a flash of white light!

"It's for the picture of the whole student body," I told Mr. Webb. "I had this idea about using the new swimming pool."

David laughed. "You want to take the picture from underwater? That's *awesome*!"

"Give me a break," I moaned. "You know they haven't filled the new pool yet. There's no water in it."

I spread my drawing out on the table, and Mr. Webb bent over to study it. He scratched his head and squinted at it. "Is that you on the high diving board?" he asked me.

I nodded. "Yeah. See? We get everyone standing in the pool. Fifth grade in front. Then sixth. Then seventh in back. And I use a wide angle and shoot down at everyone from the high board."

David giggled. "And then you dive into the crowd? Awesome!"

I ignored him.

Mr. Webb studied my drawing for a long moment. "There might be some safety problems," he said finally. "The high diving board is —"

"It's a very wide platform up there," I said. "With railings on both sides. No way I could slip."

David leaned over the drawing, blocking Mr. Webb's view. "I think Julie and I should *both* go up there and shoot," he said. "She can use her old-fashioned wide angle. And I'll use my Konica square shooter."

I wanted to pound him into the ground.

David is such a total pig.

"The platform isn't that wide," I told Mr. Webb. "There's only room for one person up there. And since it's *my* idea . . ."

"I know!" David said. "Let's make it a contest. Between Julie and me."

I swallowed. "A contest?"

"Whoever has the most pictures accepted for the yearbook — wins," David said. "The winner gets to take the big picture from the high board."

Mr. Webb thought about it. Then a thin smile crossed his needle face.

"Well, I guess that would be a fair way to decide," he said. "Okay, you have one week."

Fair?! It wasn't fair at all! The pool was *my* idea. But how could I back down?

David had a big grin on his face. I wanted to wipe it off. But I couldn't let him think I was upset. Instead, I said, "Okay. Done deal. We'll have a contest."

I folded up my plan and shoved it back into my backpack. Then I waved good-bye to the two of them and left the room.

As I walked home, I couldn't think about anything else.

I really wanted to win. I really wanted to be the one up on that high board with everyone in school looking up at me.

How was I to know that before too long I'd be falling to my doom?

3

Saturday afternoon, the sun beamed down from a clear blue sky. It was the first warm day of spring. Reena and I couldn't wait to climb on our bikes and ride all around town.

We pedaled past the school, then turned right and coasted downhill toward Fairfax Park. We were both in shorts and T-shirts. It felt great to pretend it was summer.

We had to brake to slow down at the bottom of the steep hill. "How was Sammy this morning?" Reena asked.

"The usual," I said. "He was Sammy. What else?"

Reena laughed. "Your brother is a little spoiled."

"And a little whiny," I added. "And a little obnoxious. Mom always says he's just being Sammy. I guess that means he can get away with anything."

"Baby of the family," Reena said.

We rode through the park, in and out of the shade from the old tangled trees that hang over the street. Then we rode past houses where some of our friends live.

Some kids were washing a car with a garden hose at the corner. We turned, and a red SUV pulled up beside us.

The back window rolled down. And who should poke their heads out but my best buddies, Becka and Greta.

"Ju-Ju!" they both called. "Ju-Ju!"

"You got rid of your training wheels!" Becka shouted.

Greta spit her bubble gum at me. Missed.

"Bye, Ju-Ju!" The SUV roared away with the girls laughing wildly.

I rolled my eyes and started pedaling hard. Reena raced to catch up to me, her blond hair flying behind her. "What did you ever do to them?" she asked.

"I know what it is," I said. "Remember my birthday party last fall? The bowling party?"

"I remember," Reena said. "I dropped the ball on my foot."

"Well, my mom said I could only invite five kids," I said. "And you know Becka and Greta were never in my top five. They're closer to my *bottom* five."

Reena laughed. "So you didn't invite them."

I nodded. "Right. They've been horrible to me ever since."

I slowed to a stop at a corner. The street sign was lying on its side on the grass. "Where are we?" I asked.

We both squinted into the afternoon sun. I saw tiny houses jammed close together on both sides of the block. The front yards were small squares, mostly of tall weeds.

One house had cardboard across all its windows. The yard was cluttered with tin cans and other garbage.

A mean-looking dog, tall and scrawny, barked at us from a dirt driveway, tugging at a chain leash. Two young boys were tossing stones against the side of a little shingled house.

"I don't know this neighborhood," I said. "We never rode this far before."

"It's kind of creepy," Reena said. But then her eyes grew wide. "Hey — check it out! A garage sale!"

She didn't wait for me. She pedaled up the pebble driveway where red and blue balloons bobbed in the wind.

Reena can't resist a tag sale. She's totally into old shoes and hats and vintage clothes. I don't know what she does with all the stuff she buys. It's lucky she has big closets in her room.

The redbrick house was small and square. The screen door was ripped and hung half open. A stuffed monkey stared out of the dusty front window.

A huge red-faced woman in a tight-fitting yellow dress sat in a beach chair in front of the garage. She waved to us as we climbed off our bikes, but she didn't get up.

She fanned herself with a folded-up newspaper. Then she used it to point to the tables of stuff. "Everything is half off," she said in a hoarse voice. "I didn't have time to tag it. Just ask me the price."

We set our bikes down on the pebble driveway. No one else was around. Down the block, the angry dog kept barking.

Reena walked over to a rack of old dresses and coats. It all looked pretty ragged to me. But Reena likes pawing through that stuff.

I stopped at a table in front of the open garage door. It was stacked high with yellowed, old *Time* magazines and sheet music.

I picked up some sheet music and looked through it. My dad plays the piano, and he collects old songs. But these were too smelly and falling apart. Yuck.

I dropped them back on the table, but my hands still smelled skunky.

I turned and saw Reena trying on straw hats. She's so awesome looking, hats look great on her. Whenever I try one of hers on, I look like a little girl playing dress up.

There were shelves of old board games and action figures in the garage. I checked out an old werewolf card game called *Bite My Face!* Really dumb.

Then in the gray light at the back of the garage, I spotted something on a low shelf. A camera.

I bent and picked it up. "Weird," I muttered.

It was definitely old. It was square, like an old box camera. Bigger than my digital camera, and heavier. It was metal, covered in black leather. I turned it over and saw a built-in flash at the top.

"Wonder what kind of film it takes," I muttered. I'd never seen a camera like it.

I had five or ten dollars in my backpack. Would that be enough to buy the old camera?

I carried it up to the woman in the beach chair. "Is this for sale?" I asked.

The woman's eyes bulged. Her chins trembled.

"NO!" she screamed. "Put it DOWN! You don't *want* that! Put it down — NOW!"

4

"N-no problem," I stammered.

The woman was waving me away with both hands. Her face was beet-red.

I turned and trotted back into the garage, the camera still in my hands. *What's up with this camera?* I wondered.

I bent to set it back down on the low shelf — and felt a tap on my shoulder.

"Huh?" I let out a startled cry. Turned — and saw a girl standing behind me. She was about twelve like me, big and red-faced like the woman outside.

Her scraggly brown hair fell over her eyes. She wore baggy jeans and a pink sweatshirt that said MOMMY'S PRINCESS on the front in sparkly letters.

"You want that camera?" she whispered.

"Well . . . I don't know," I murmured. "If there's something wrong with it . . ."

She shoved it against my chest. "Go ahead. Take it."

"How much?" I asked.

The girl shook her head. "No charge. Just take it away before my mom sees." She gave me a push toward the driveway.

I picked up my bike and stuck the old camera into my backpack. The woman didn't see. She was pouring herself a tall drink from a big plastic pitcher.

Reena ran over and lifted her bike from the driveway. "Nothing good here," she whispered. "Let's go."

We called "bye" to the woman and pedaled away. At the street, I turned and looked back to the garage. The daughter was standing there stiffly, just staring at us.

I waved to her. But she didn't wave back.

Mom greeted us as we stepped into my house. My mom is dark-haired like me, except she wears hers the length of bristles on a hairbrush. She's short and a little chubby and has nonstop energy. I mean, she never sits down.

"Reena, would you like to stay for dinner?" she asked.

"Sure, thanks," Reena replied.

"What are we having?" I asked.

Mom shrugged. "Just pizza. I've been cleaning the attic all day. No time to prepare a feast."

That's the other thing about my mom. She never sits down — and she never stops cleaning out rooms.

"No peppers this time!" Sammy came bursting into the room, whining as usual. "I hate peppers! Even if you pull them off, you can still taste them."

Sammy looks like a junior version of Mom and me. He's short with dark hair and has brown eyes and a gap in his front teeth — like I had before my braces.

"Okay. No peppers," Mom promised.

I pulled the old camera from my backpack. I was eager to check it out.

"Where'd you get that?" Sammy asked. He made a grab for it, but I swiped it out of his reach.

"Take my picture!" he demanded. He posed against the fireplace, stuck his tongue out, and crossed his eyes. "Hurry! Take my picture."

"It doesn't have any film," I said. "I just got it. Besides, when I do get film, I'm taking Reena's picture — not yours."

I turned and aimed the lens at Reena. Then I pretended to take her picture and pushed the shutter button.

The flash went off — a bright white. I heard a metal hum — and a square of paper came sliding out of the front of the camera.

"What's *that*?" Sammy cried. "You broke it! Ha-ha! You broke your new camera!" He did a little dance around Reena and me.

I pulled out the square. It was cardboard and had a smooth, glossy front.

"Julie didn't break it," Mom said. "Haven't you ever seen one of these? It's a *self-developing* camera."

"A *what*?" Sammy said.

"Watch. The picture slides out. Then it will slowly develop," Mom said. "These used to be popular before digital cameras."

We all stared at the little square in my hand. It began to darken. Then colors appeared. Slowly, the picture developed, and we could see Reena.

"Nice colors," I said. "Very soft. This is awesome!"

"Oh, wow," Reena groaned. "It's a nice shot — but I have red-eye."

I studied the photo. Yes, Reena looked great. I don't think she can take a bad picture. But her eyes were glowing bright red.

Sammy laughed at Reena. "You look like a *freak*!" Then he grabbed for the camera again. "Let *me* take a picture!"

I spun away from him. "It isn't a toy, Sammy." I tugged Reena to the stairs. "Come to my room. Bet I can get rid of the red-eye."

"On the computer?" Reena asked.

I nodded. "Yes. I'll scan the picture into my computer and fix the red-eye."

We hurried up to my room and closed the door so Sammy wouldn't follow us.

I scanned the picture into the computer. I have a professional program called PhotoMaster Plus I'm learning how to use.

I gazed at the picture on the screen and began to adjust it. "Weird," I muttered.

"What's up?" Reena asked. She put her hands on my shoulders and leaned over me.

"I can't darken your eyes," I said. "I should be able to fade the red glow. But it won't adjust at all."

"OH, HELP! OWWWWW! MY EYES —!" Reena shrieked.

I gasped and spun around.

Reena raised her hands to her eyes. And started to scream at the top of her lungs. "MY EYES! HELP ME! MY EYES!"

I let out another gasp. And jumped up from the chair. "What's *wrong*?"

Reena pressed her hands over her eyes. "HELP ME! Julie — my eyes are BURNING! Oh, HELP ME!"

I grabbed her hands gently and tugged them down. When I saw her eyes, my breath caught in my throat.

Her eyes were glowing red like fire!

"Help me!" she moaned. "Oh, it hurts! It *really* hurts!"

"M-maybe the flash was too bright," I stammered. "You were standing so close to the camera."

I pulled Reena into my bathroom. I soaked a washcloth with cold water and pressed it over her eyes.

"It isn't helping!" she shrieked. "My eyes — they're BURNING! It hurts SO MUCH!"

I took the cloth away. Her eyes were still glowing bright red.

"Here. More cold water," I said. I placed the washcloth back on her face. Then I pulled her downstairs to Mom. "Her eyes are burning. They're all red," I told her.

"Let me see." Mom pulled the cloth away. She blinked a few times when she saw the red glow. "Something irritated them badly," she said. "Do you have allergies?"

Reena shook her head. Her whole body was trembling. "NO! No allergies! Please — HELP ME!"

"I have some eye drops in my room," Mom said. "Julie, they're on my dresser."

We tried the eye drops. They didn't help at all.

"Call Reena's parents," Mom said. "Maybe they can get her to an eye doctor. I've never seen anything like this!"

Mrs. Jacobs arrived a few minutes later. We helped Reena into the car. "Call me later," I said. "When the burning stops."

I watched them drive away. I had a tight feeling in my stomach. I couldn't get Reena's frightened screams out of my ears.

In my bedroom, I picked up the snapshot. I stared at Reena's smiling face with the red, glowing eyes.

How totally weird, I thought.

After dinner, I was still thinking about Reena. I suddenly remembered I had an assignment from Mr. Webb. I was supposed to be at the gym, shooting the girls' basketball game for the yearbook.

I grabbed two of my cameras and stuffed them in my bag. Then I jumped on my bike and raced to the gym.

I got there just in time. The game was nearly over. Our Tigers were losing to the Bay Meadow Stingrays.

I saw Karla Mayer, our best player. She stole the ball and dribbled down the floor. She stopped at the line and sent up an easy three-pointer.

The bleachers were about half full of kids. Most of them started to stomp their feet and chant, "Karla kills! Karla kills! Karla kills!"

I decided to take some shots from the top of the bleachers. I took out my best digital camera and hurried up the steep steps. I let out a sharp cry as a red-and-white sneaker stuck out and tripped me.

"Ow." I fell and banged my knee hard. I turned and saw who was wearing the sneaker — Becka. She and Greta grinned at me.

"Not too klutzy, are you?" Becka said. She laughed.

"Ju-Ju, too bad. Did you fall on your camera?" Greta shouted over the noise of the crowd.

I should have ignored them. Instead, I said, "Becka, don't you have awfully big feet for a girl?"

Then I glanced at my camera. Oh, wow. I really *did* fall on it. The lens was cracked.

Shaking my head, I climbed to the top of the bleachers.

I gazed at the scoreboard. The Tigers were losing 36 to 45. Karla would have to go to work. Good photo ops.

I reached into my bag for the other camera — and let out a cry. "Oh, no!" The weird, old camera. I didn't mean to bring it.

Well . . . I had no choice. I had to use it.

I knew I couldn't snap dozens of shots with the old thing. I needed to wait for one or two great moments.

I *had* to get a long shot of Karla running down the floor. Could the old camera do it? I raised it to my face — then groaned.

David Blank! He had a blue baseball cap pulled down over his red hair. But I still recognized him easily.

What was *he* doing here?

David was on the floor next to the players' bench. He had two cameras strapped around his neck. And he was snapping photo after photo.

25

"You creep!" I shouted out loud. He *knew* this was my assignment.

David would do *anything* to win our contest. But this just wasn't fair.

The Stingrays scored again. The crowd grew quiet. Everyone was waiting for Karla to make a move.

I glanced down the bleachers. Becka was on her cell phone. Greta was searching for something in her bag. They weren't even watching the game.

I held the old camera ready. A few seconds later, Karla came dribbling full speed down the center of the floor.

This was my shot. I kept her in the view screen as she flew toward the basket. She leaped high and sent a layup to the hoop.

I pushed the shutter button just as her feet left the floor. The camera flashed. The square of film came sliding out.

I gazed at the photo, watching it develop.

"Weird!" I cried. "How did I mess up?"

The picture showed Karla's arm all by itself.

Where was the rest of her body? Her face?

How could I just capture her arm?

A loud *CRAAAAACK* made the kids in the bleachers gasp.

And rising over that, I heard a high wail, a long, shrill scream of pain.

I turned — and saw Karla dangling from the basket rim.

Hanging by her arm!

Karla shrieked and cried. Tears rolled down her face.

Even from the top of the bleachers, I could see that her arm was horribly broken. It hung there at a totally strange angle.

Players from both teams stood beneath her, screaming and crying. Kids were covering their eyes. The coaches hurried to lower her to the floor.

The referee kept blowing her whistle, again and again, like a siren.

Wailing in agony, Karla lay sprawled on her back on the gym floor, the bones of her arm poking out through her skin.

Gasping for breath, I realized I had the snapshot clenched tightly in my hand. I raised it to my face and stared at it.

Stared at Karla's arm, all by itself.

And suddenly, I felt sick.

Four paramedics in white uniforms arrived a short while later. They couldn't keep the shock off their faces when they saw Karla. Coach Ambers was down on the floor beside her, trying to hold Karla still.

Karla was silent now. I thought maybe she was in shock or something.

The gym had emptied out. Both teams had been sent to the locker rooms.

The medics lifted Karla onto a stretcher. I could see that her arm was bent almost backwards.

I tucked the photo into my bag. The referee had left the gym. But I could still hear her shrill whistle ringing in my ear.

I thought about Reena. About her red-eye. And then I pictured Karla's arm again.

A deep shudder ran down my body.

Maybe I should have listened to that woman's warning.

Maybe I should have left the camera in her garage.

This CAN'T be a coincidence! There's something evil about this old camera....

I didn't see David until he was right in front of me. He grabbed the old camera from my hand.

"Hey!" I cried out, and tried to take it back.

But he swiped it out of my reach. "Whoa! This is totally awesome!" he said. "Where did you get this? Let me try it!"

"NO!" I screamed. I made another grab for it.

Too late.

David aimed the camera at *me* — and FLASHED it in my face.

I shut my eyes. I could still see the white flash with my eyes closed.

I heard the film slide out from the camera.

When I opened my eyes, David was staring at the camera. He laughed. "Is this a toy? This is Sammy's camera, right?"

"It's very old," I said. "I have to take it back. There's something wrong with it."

David rolled it around in his hand. "Look. Something popped out of it. Does it squirt water, too?"

"You're not funny," I said. And then I saw what he was looking at. The square of film. It didn't slide all the way out. It was stuck halfway in the camera.

"See? It's broken," I said. "I'm going to return it —"

I stopped. My breath caught in my throat.

A sharp pain wrapped around my middle.

It felt as if I were wearing a heavy belt. And

the belt kept tightening and tightening . . . and tightening.

I made a groaning sound.

I couldn't breathe.

I doubled over. The pain shot around me.

I felt as if I'd been *cut in half*!

"Julie? Julie?" I felt David's hands on my shoulders. "Are you okay? What's wrong?"

I couldn't straighten up. I couldn't talk. Or breathe.

Cut in half . . . cut in half . . .

Suddenly, I realized what I had to do.

Fighting the pain, I struggled to raise myself. I grabbed the camera.

The pain tightened around my middle.

"Julie? Do you need help?"

I could hear David's voice. It sounded far away.

"Julie? Does something hurt?" he cried. "Should I get someone?"

I couldn't answer. The pain tightened my jaw, tightened every muscle.

I saw red. Then black. I knew I was about to pass out.

Gritting my teeth, I grabbed the film square. And I tugged it hard, pulled it the rest of the way out of the camera.

Will it work?

Will the pain go away now?

I gritted my teeth and waited . . . waited . . .

No.

The photo fell from my hand. I bent double, squeezing my sides. The pain tightened around me. It felt like a hot wire burning into my skin.

And then . . . the pain vanished.

It didn't fade away slowly. It just disappeared. So suddenly, I gasped and jerked up straight, blinking in surprise.

I took in a long, deep breath, then another. I rubbed a hand around my waist. It felt perfectly fine again.

"Are you okay now?" David asked. He had gone so pale, his freckles had faded into his skin. "Julie?"

I didn't answer. I gripped the camera tightly against my chest. Then I spun away from David and ran across the gym floor.

"Hey!" David shouted after me. "What's your problem?"

I didn't answer. I kept running until I was outside in the parking lot, breathing in the cool, fresh night air.

I *knew* what my problem was. It was the camera.

First Reena, then Karla . . . then me.

The camera was evil. It hurt people.

I had to get rid of it. I had to take it back to that strange woman.

I held the camera tightly against me and pedaled my bike home, riding with one hand. A car rolled past with loud music pouring out of the open windows. A girl waved to me from the passenger seat. But I didn't wave back.

I tossed my bike against the side of the garage. Breathing hard, I ran into the house through the kitchen door.

I planned to hurry up to my room and hide the camera before anyone saw me. But Sammy jumped out as I stepped into the living room. He had an ugly rubber skeleton mask over his face.

"Take my picture — or you die!" he rasped. He struck a pose with both hands raised and curled like claws.

"Sammy, since when is it Halloween?" I asked.

"I'm not Sammy. I'm the Silver Skull. Take my picture. Or I'll crush you with my Skull Vision."

I shuddered. Poor Sammy. If I took his picture with this evil camera, he probably *would* become a skeleton!

"Out of my way." I didn't mean to push him so hard. But I was desperate to get the camera hidden away in my room.

"Hey — you're skeleton meat!" Sammy shouted, waving his fist angrily. "You will feel the wrath of the Silver Skull!"

That made me laugh. He's a spoiled brat, but he's cute.

I crossed my room and pulled open the closet door. In the back, I had a tall heap of dirty clothes that I'd forgotten about.

I buried the camera under the mountain of jeans and shirts. *No way* Sammy would find it there.

My heart was pounding like a drum. I knew I wouldn't feel normal again until I returned the evil thing. At least it couldn't do any more harm buried under a ton of smelly clothes.

I dropped onto my bed with a weary sigh. I pulled my cell phone out, clicked it open, and called Reena. "Are your eyes better?" I asked.

"No, they're not," Reena answered sharply. "All thanks to you!"

"Excuse me?"

"You heard me," Reena snapped. "My eyes are still glowing like a freak. And still burning."

"Oh, I'm so sorry," I moaned.

"I can't read. I can't watch TV. I can't do my homework!" Reena shouted. "And I can't go to school because I can't let anyone see me like this!"

"Reena, I'm really sorry —" I repeated.

"Sorry?" Reena cried. "Sorry? Julie, that woman *warned* you not to take the camera. But you think you know it all. You think you can do whatever you want. Well . . . look what you did to me!"

"Reena, please —" I begged.

"The doctor never saw anything like this!" Reena screamed. "You — you ruined my life, Julie!"

"But — why are you talking to me like this?" I cried. "We're friends and —"

"No, we're not," Reena replied. "We're not friends anymore. No way."

I couldn't believe she said that. I realized my whole body was trembling. I could barely hold the phone to my ear.

I could hear her sobbing into the phone.

"Reena, listen to me," I pleaded. "I'm taking the camera back to that house tomorrow. Will you come with me? We can ask that woman about your eyes."

"Julie, get lost!" Reena said in a low, cold voice. And she clicked off her phone.

The next day, school dragged on forever. I kept thinking about the camera hidden away in my closet. And I really missed Reena.

Her telling me to get lost tied my stomach in knots every time I thought about it.

After school, I ran all the way home. I wanted to get there before Sammy.

I dove into my closet and tossed the dirty clothes aside. Then I grabbed the camera and headed to the garage to get my bike.

Wouldn't you know it? Flat tire.

I didn't care. The camera was going to be returned today if I had to crawl!

I stuffed it into my backpack and started to walk. A cool wind blew in my face. It made the tall trees in the front yards sway and creak. The sun kept disappearing behind dark clouds.

I was pretty sure I remembered how to get there. I walked past my school. Some boys from my class were tossing Frisbees on the front lawn.

Past the school, I turned and walked down the steep hill toward Fairfax Park. A few kids I didn't recognize were taking turns skateboarding down the hill.

I wished I was having fun, too.

I felt a couple of cold raindrops on my forehead as I stepped into the park. The dark clouds spread across the sky. The wind grew colder.

Turn around, a voice in my head whispered. *Julie, go home.*

"No!" I said out loud. I kept walking.

The trees swayed and whispered as I made my way through the park. The wind swirled, but the rain held off.

I hurried through the park. Then walked through a neighborhood of small, square houses.

Was I on the right street? Yes. I could see the woman's redbrick house halfway down the next block.

I waited for a yellow school bus to pass. Then I started to cross the street.

I took a few steps and stopped when I heard a cough behind me.

I spun around. No one there.

Weird.

I crossed the rest of the way. I started to walk faster since I could see the house. Almost there!

But I stopped again when I heard the scrape of footsteps. Soft thuds on the sidewalk.

Again, I turned. The street was lined with slender young trees.

Did someone slip behind one of them?

I turned and took a few more steps. I was almost to the woman's driveway. I heard more soft footsteps behind me.

A chill shot down my back.

I'm being followed.

Rain started to fall. I spun around. My eyes darted from tree to tree.

"Who's there?" I called. My voice sounded muffled by the rain.

No answer.

"I know you're there!" I shouted. "Who is it?"

No reply.

I shivered. I lowered my head against the rain and ran up the pebble driveway.

The garage door was closed. Someone had scrawled a big red X on the front. I turned and saw the stuffed monkey staring out the front window. Behind the stuffed animal, the house was dark.

Raindrops pattered the window. They sounded like soft drumbeats.

I glanced behind me. I didn't see anyone. But I knew someone was there, watching me. It wasn't my imagination.

With another shiver, I rang the doorbell. I could hear it echo inside the house.

I waited a few seconds. Then rang it again. No answer.

I pulled open the torn screen door. Then I raised my fist and knocked hard on the front door.

The door swung open.

I peeked inside. "Hello?" I shouted. "Anyone home? Hello?"

Silence. Just the patter of rain behind me.

I stepped inside into the small, square living room. I squinted into the darkness — and gasped.

The room was totally bare. No furniture at all. The stuffed monkey sat on the windowsill. Nothing else in the room. Not even a rug on the floor.

"Hello?" I shouted. "Anybody here?"

My voice echoed in the empty room. I jogged into the kitchen. Nothing in there, either. A single pot stood on the stove, its insides burned black. Even the sink faucet had been taken away.

With a sigh, I leaned against the wall. Rainwater dripped down my forehead. I brushed it off with the back of one hand.

They moved away, I realized.

The woman and her daughter had a garage sale and then cleared out.

"Now what?" I asked myself out loud.

I gripped the evil camera in both hands. No way I could return it to them now.

So what should I do with it?

I can't take it home, I told myself.

It didn't take me long to decide to leave it there. I started to feel better as soon as I made the decision.

Back in the living room, I turned the stuffed monkey around. And I lowered the camera to its lap.

I backed away. I had a smile on my face. It felt so good to leave the camera. The monkey's stare seemed to follow me as I backed out the door.

I closed the front door and then the screen door. The rain had stopped. The sun was breaking out through the clouds.

Things were looking better already!

Back home, I had a couple of hours before dinnertime. I felt too restless to sit down and do my homework.

I grabbed my digital camera, my extra lens, and headed to school. I needed to take some interesting shots for the yearbook. *No way* was I going to let David win our contest!

I found some kids Rollerblading to loud hip-hop music in the teachers' parking lot. I took some good shots of them. I tried to capture how much fun they were having.

Then I photographed a bunch of seventh-graders playing a kickball game on the soccer field. It was a pretty out-of-control game. The grass was still wet from the rain, and they kept slipping and sliding and falling on their butts.

Some good snaps.

"David, you're toast," I muttered to myself as I headed home.

I couldn't wait to download the photos onto my computer. Then I'd print them and bring the best ones to Mr. Webb tomorrow.

Mom and Dad were in the kitchen. Dad was at the sink, peeling carrots. Mom was stirring something on the stove.

"What's up?" Dad asked. Then he let out a shout. "Ouch! Can't they make a carrot peeler that doesn't scrape your fingers to shreds?" He raised his hand. "Look! I'm bleeding!"

Dad isn't real good in the kitchen. I don't know why he keeps volunteering to help.

"About ten minutes till dinnertime," Mom said.

"No problem," I said. "Dad, do you need a Band-Aid?"

"I need ten!" he cried. But he kept scraping away.

I hurried up to my room. I carried the digital camera to my desk and set it down next to my computer.

Something caught my eye. I spun around — and uttered a shocked cry. "Nooooo — !"

The stuffed monkey! It sat on my dresser with the evil camera on its lap!

"But . . . that's *impossible*!" I cried.

I shut my eyes tight, then opened them again. The monkey and the camera were still there.

How did they get there? *How?*

My chest felt fluttery. My heart was racing. I grabbed the camera and bolted down the stairs with it.

I burst into the kitchen, breathing hard. "Mom? Dad? Was someone here?" I cried.

They both looked up from the counter. "Someone?"

"In my room," I said. "Was someone in my room?"

Sammy poked his head out from under the table. "Yeah. The Silver Skull was there!" he exclaimed. "The Silver Skull goes everywhere!"

"Give me a break," I snapped. "I'm serious!"

Mom shook her head. "I've been here all afternoon, Julie. I didn't see or hear anyone. Were you expecting someone?"

"No," I said. "It's . . . hard to explain. I —"

No way I could expect them to believe me about the camera. They're both accountants for an insurance company.

Know what that means? It means they're the kind of people who don't believe in evil cameras.

Sammy jumped out from under the table. He dropped the two action figures he'd been playing with. He tore over to me and tried to grab the camera out of my hands.

"Give it," he said. "Give it up. I want to try it."

I used the camera to push him away. "Here's a new concept for you," I said. "It's called *mine* and *yours*. Do you know the difference between *mine* and *yours*? Did they ever teach that to you on *Sesame Street*?"

"You're a jerkface baboon," Sammy said.

"Don't call names," Dad told him.

"Why won't you let Sammy try your camera?" Mom asked. "He isn't going to break it."

"Yes, I am!" Sammy said. Talk about a jerk-face baboon!

I didn't answer Mom. I spun around and ran back up to my room with it.

I hid it again under the pile of dirty clothes. But I knew that wasn't good enough. My little brother is a terrible snoop. I knew he'd find it. I knew that sooner or later, he'd get into terrible trouble with it.

I had to get the evil thing out of the house. I had to put it someplace where it couldn't magically return.

But . . . where would that be?

Where?

11

It was nearly bedtime, but I wasn't tired. I kept picturing the camera on the floor of my closet. I couldn't stop thinking about Reena and Karla. About the horrible pain the camera had given me.

I knew I wouldn't sleep until the evil thing was removed from the house.

I tiptoed to the closet. I didn't want Mom or Dad to hear me.

The floor creaked under my feet. The only sound except for the swish of the filmy white curtains fluttering at my open window.

I peered out at a purple sky with no moon or stars. A soft breeze made the dark trees shiver. Somewhere down the block, a cat cried. A mournful sound. Poor kitty probably wanted to go inside.

I didn't want to be outside, either. But I knew what I had to do. I had a plan.

I crossed the room in the dark, got down on my knees in the closet, and grabbed the evil camera. My hands were trembling, and my knees felt weak as I sneaked down the stairs.

A few seconds later, I silently closed the kitchen door behind me. I waited for my eyes to adjust to the dark. The cool, damp air felt good on my face.

The neighbors' houses were all dark. Down the block, the cat continued its sad cry. Again, I searched the sky for the moon. But it was hidden behind a heavy blanket of clouds.

I crossed my backyard and followed the narrow dirt alley behind the houses. The ground was soft and muddy from the rain. My shoes splashed into shallow mud puddles.

I pressed the camera against my chest and kept walking. A few minutes later, I stopped in front of Alley Pond.

That's what everyone calls it. It doesn't really have a name. It's a small, round pond at the end of the alley.

Some kids say it used to be a fishpond. Not anymore. It's a big, round hole filled with muddy water.

I raised the camera and prepared to toss it into the pond.

But I stopped when I heard a sound.

A scraping sound. From behind a thorny hedge at the side of the alley.

I spun around quickly.

Did I hear *breathing* from behind the hedge? Or just the wind?

A chill tightened the back of my neck. Again, I had the feeling that someone was there. Someone was watching me.

"Hello?" I called out in a whisper. "Who's there?"

No answer.

Another chill shook my body. I could feel all my muscles tighten.

Was someone watching me? I was really afraid now. But I had to finish my mission.

I raised my arm again — and heaved the old camera into the pond.

It made a big, thudding splash. Then it sank below the muddy surface instantly.

I stared at the pond for a few seconds. It didn't float back up.

I glanced one more time at the low hedge. No one there. Silence.

Was it my imagination?

I ran back to the house, splashing up mud with my sneakers. I silently let myself into the kitchen. Then crept back upstairs.

I stopped halfway down the hall. I saw yellow light seeping from my half-closed bedroom door.

There was someone in my room!

12

My heart thudded in my chest. I tiptoed to the door. Slowly, carefully, I tilted my head forward to peek into my room.

"Sammy!" I gasped.

Sammy spun around at the sound of my voice. He was in his pajamas. On his knees in front of my dresser. He had the bottom dresser drawer pulled out.

I stepped into the room. "What are you doing in here?" I cried.

"I heard you go out," he replied. "I wanted to look at your camera."

I slammed the dresser drawer shut. Then I pulled him to his feet. "You little sneak," I muttered. I gave him a push to the door.

"I just wanted to try it," he whined.

"Forget about that camera," I said. "It's gone, Sammy. It's gone forever." I gave him another push.

He tried to kick me. But his bare foot caught

on the edge of the carpet. "If you didn't want it, why didn't you give it to me?" he asked.

"It was broken," I told him. "I had to throw it away."

He started to argue. But I closed the bedroom door in his face.

I yawned. I suddenly felt totally exhausted. All my muscles ached. My head felt like a heavy rock.

It still took a long time to fall asleep. And when I finally did, I had a disturbing dream.

I dreamed I was on the high diving board at the new swimming pool. Everyone in school was jammed into the pool, staring up at me. I was ready to take the big yearbook photo.

I raised the evil camera in both hands. It didn't feel like a camera. It felt soft and warm.

As I gripped it, I could feel it moving in my hands ... throbbing ... *breathing*!

The camera was ALIVE!

I held it in front of my face. I tried to look through the viewfinder. The camera began breathing harder. In and out ...

Something splattered onto my shoes. I glanced down. I saw drops of blood.

The camera lens was bleeding. Bright red blood. Drip after drip.

But I still kept taking pictures. I aimed the camera down at the kids below. And I clicked the shutter.

I held the film in my hand and watched as the picture developed. It took a long, long time.

I gasped when the shot finally came into focus. In the picture, the kids' skin had vanished. Their skulls gleamed in the sunlight. They were all *skeletons*.

"What have I *done*?" I screamed. "Have I killed everyone in my entire school?"

I woke up drenched in sweat. I tried to blink the dream away. But the grinning, glowing skeletons stayed in my mind.

"Only a dream," I muttered. "Take a deep breath, Julie. It was only a dream."

I shut my eyes and settled back on the pillow. I couldn't stop shivering. I knew I wouldn't fall back to sleep.

I just lay there staring up at the ceiling. After a while, the sun started to rise outside my window. It sent a warm, rosy color over the room.

I climbed out of bed and crossed to the window. I watched the sunrise, letting the warmth flow over me. I started to feel better.

I got dressed for school. Then I made my way downstairs for breakfast.

I was the first one in the kitchen. I started for the fridge to pull out the orange juice.

But I stopped halfway across the floor. And stared.

Stared at the evil camera, sitting by my place at the breakfast table.

13

The camera was dripping wet. The lens was covered in mud.

I wanted to scream. I wanted to heave the thing against the wall again and again. Jump up and down on it. Crush it with a hammer.

But I knew it was no use.

I left it in that house way across town. I tossed it into the pond.

But here it was. No way. No way to get rid of it.

I snatched it off the table. Then I ran upstairs and hid it in my closet before anyone came down to breakfast.

I couldn't think of anything else all day.

At noon, the Sneer Sisters — Becka and Greta — tripped me and made me spill my lunch tray on the floor. Laughter rang out in the lunchroom.

"Watch where you're going," Becka said with a sneer.

I didn't pay any attention. I didn't even look at the two of them. I just walked out of the lunchroom without eating.

I kept picturing the camera on the breakfast table. My stomach felt tight, as if it were twisted into a dozen knots. I could barely swallow. How could I eat?

I knew I had to get help.

After school, I loaded the camera into my backpack. I rode my bike to the mall. I parked it in a bike rack and trotted to the Camera World store on the second floor.

The bell over the door chimed as I stepped in. I saw David's dad standing behind the glass display counter. He wore a blue-and-white-striped shirt and khakis. He was polishing a big camera lens with a soft white cloth.

He smiled when he recognized me. "Julie? How's it going?"

Mr. Blank is short and thin. He has a narrow, almost bald head with a fringe of black hair at his ears. He has brown eyes, a nice smile, and a black mustache that looks like two tiny straight lines under his nose.

"I want to show you something," I said. I tugged the camera from my backpack and set it down on the glass counter. "Can you tell me anything about this weird old camera?"

He set the lens down carefully. Then he folded

the cloth and tucked it into a drawer. "Let me see this thing," he said.

He picked it up in one hand and twirled it slowly in front of his face. "Weird old camera is right," he muttered. "Where did you get it, Julie? Did you find it on eBay?"

"Garage sale," I said.

"I don't think I've seen one like it before," he said. He turned it over and studied the bottom. "No brand name," he said. "No ID numbers anywhere."

He looked through the viewfinder. Then he studied the lens. "It's self-developing," he said. "That's very unusual in a camera this old."

"It's . . . a very unusual camera," I said.

Mr. Blank stroked his mustache. "I have some books and old catalogs in the office," he said. "Let's look it up."

I followed him into the little office in back. It was the size of a broom closet. It had a desk with a computer on it, a chair, and stacks and stacks of camera books and magazines.

Mr. Blank pulled some fat old books from the bottom of a pile and started thumbing through them. "No name on the camera makes it a lot harder to find," he said.

He cracked open another old book and began sifting through it. "I'm an expert on old cameras," he said. "People say I have a photographic memory. Ha-ha. That's a bad joke, isn't it? But I've never seen . . . oh, wait!"

He squinted at a photo on the page of the old book. "I think maybe . . ." His eyes darted back and forth as he read the tiny type.

Finally, he gazed up at me. "Julie, I think you've found something very rare," he said. He raised the camera and compared it to the photo. "Yes. Yes . . ."

"What is it?" I asked.

"It says that only *one* of these cameras was ever built," Mr. Blank said. "It was actually made for a horror movie that was being filmed in the 1950s."

I swallowed. "A horror movie?"

He nodded. "The camera was made for a movie called *Say Cheese — and Die Screaming!*" He read the tiny text again. "But the movie was never finished. There were a lot of strange accidents on the set, and they had to close down the production."

I felt a chill. "Bad things?"

Mr. Blank shrugged. "That's all it says. The movie was never finished. And the camera disappeared."

He closed the book. "Lucky you," he said. "I think you found a piece of movie history." He started to hand the camera back to me.

"No. P-please," I stammered. I backed away. "Can you keep it?"

He blinked. "Excuse me? This camera is probably valuable, Julie. It —"

"There's something very wrong with it," I said. My voice came out high and shrill. "I don't want it. Please —"

"It can be repaired," he said.

"No, it can't!" I cried. "There's a curse on it or something. The camera is EVIL! Please, Mr. Blank — take it. Keep it safe. Keep it away from people."

He squinted at me. "I don't believe in curses or magic," he said. "That's crazy."

"Please — just take it," I said. I turned to go.

"Maybe I could give you store credit," he said. "You could pick something out in return."

"No thanks!" I said. I couldn't stay there another second. I just wanted to get away from the camera.

I bolted out of the office and out the front door. The bell over the door clanged loudly. I ran into the mall. Nearly knocked over a woman pushing a double baby stroller. "Sorry," I called, and kept running.

Did I actually get rid of that evil thing? I wondered.

Will it be safe with Mr. Blank?

Or will it come back to haunt me again?

After school the next day, I pulled my digital camera from my locker. Then I hurried to the auditorium. Kids were rehearsing a play, *Bye Bye Birdie*, and I planned to photograph it for the yearbook.

Everyone was huddled in front of the curtain. Mrs. Harper sat at the piano at the side of the stage. She was banging out a number from the show.

She is the new music teacher. She told us all she wants to shake things up around our school.

Bye Bye Birdie is the biggest musical our middle school ever tried. I planned to take hundreds of shots, from the beginning rehearsals to opening night.

But as I hurried toward the stage, I let out a groan. I'd totally forgotten that Becka and Greta were in the play.

They stood in the middle of the stage, arguing with each other about something. But as soon as they saw me, they both turned and made ugly faces.

I made a face back at them. Then I heard heavy footsteps behind me. Shoes thudding on the concrete auditorium floor.

I spun around.

"David!" I cried. "What are *you* doing here?"

He had a big grin on his face. He swung his hands from behind his back — and I stared at what he was carrying. The evil camera!

He raised it to his face, turned to the stage,

and aimed it up at Becka and Greta. "Say cheese!" he called up to them.

I froze in horror.

He raised his thumb to push the shutter button.

"NOOOOOOO!" I screamed.

14

I stuck my hand in front of the lens.

David lowered the camera. "Why did you do that?" he cried. "What's your problem, Julie?"

I didn't answer. I stomped toward him and made him back up in the aisle. "What are you doing with that camera?" I demanded.

David shrugged. "What's the big deal? My dad let me borrow it. He said you didn't want it anymore."

"But — but —" I sputtered.

"I *know* you tried to get rid of it," David said.

"Huh?" My breath caught in my throat. "How do you know that?"

He shrugged again. "I watched you," he said softly. A strange smile spread over his face. "I followed you, Julie."

"You WHAT?" I cried.

"Who do you think was spying on you?" David said, still grinning. "I stayed up day and night. I watched you leave it in that little house. And

I watched you toss it in the pond. Who do you think returned it to you both times?"

My mouth hung open. "How did you get it from the bottom of the pond?" I asked.

"I reached in and pulled it out." David laughed. "That pond is only a foot deep."

I just stared at him. I couldn't speak.

"You sneaked into my house? You returned it? You *spied* on me? But — *why*?" I cried.

"Just to mess with your mind," David replied. "I really want to win our contest, Julie. I wanted to get you totally stressed so I could win it easily."

I gave a bitter laugh. "Well, you got me totally stressed, David," I said. "Good work, dude." And then I added, "But I'm still going to win the contest."

He started to say something. But Becka interrupted from the stage. "David — take our picture for the yearbook!"

Becka and Greta both started waving David to the stage.

I stepped in front of David and raised my digital camera. "I'll do it," I said. "I was here first."

"But we don't *want* you to snap us," Greta said nastily.

"Yeah, Ju-Ju. You don't know how to snap *bubble gum*!" Becka exclaimed.

They both laughed and slapped high fives. Like that was some kind of hilarious joke.

"Go away, Ju-Ju," Greta said. "David has the cool camera."

I turned to David. "Don't use that camera," I said. "I'm warning you."

He laughed. "Warning me?"

"I had a good reason to get rid of it," I said. "David, listen —"

But he raised the camera in both hands. And aimed it at the two girls.

"No!" I dove forward. Tried to grab it away from him.

Too late.

The camera flashed. The film slid out.

"An instant classic!" David cried. He handed the picture up to Becka.

She and Greta leaned over it, watching it develop.

They had smiles on their faces. But the smiles quickly faded.

"Ohhh, gross!" Becka cried.

Greta groaned, too. "Oh, that's totally SICK!"

15

The two girls squinted at the photo.

"What's wrong with your camera, Ju-Ju?" Becka asked. "The color is all messed up."

"Huh? *My* camera?" I cried. "David was the one —"

"Your camera stinks!" Greta said. "Like *you*, Ju-Ju!"

"Why are you blaming *me*?" I said. "I didn't —"

But Becka shoved the picture into my face. David and I stared at it.

In the snapshot, both girls had green faces and arms. And their skin was all cracked and spotted — *like alligator skin*!

I gasped.

Was that going to happen to Becka and Greta?

Were they both going to get green alligator skin in a few minutes?

A shudder shook my body. I nearly lost my lunch.

David had snapped the picture. But the two girls blamed *me*. They blamed my camera. Not David.

If the picture came true . . .

I shuddered again.

I knew I had to get help. But who could help me? Mom and Dad would never believe a wild story like this.

I grabbed the camera from David. And I ran up the aisle to the exit.

I could hear the two girls making jokes about my camera. Then suddenly, the jokes stopped.

I reached the auditorium doors. I started to push one open.

And I heard two shrill screams of horror. From the stage.

I didn't have to turn around. I knew what I would see.

My knees felt weak. I grabbed the door handle to hold myself up. Another shudder ran down my body.

I turned slowly — and saw Becka and Greta screaming and tugging at their faces.

Even from the back of the auditorium, I could see their dry green skin. All cracked and lined and lumpy.

I swallowed hard. I forced myself to breathe.

Becka shook a fist at me. "YOU did this to us!" she shrieked. "You're a WITCH!"

"Why do you HATE us SO MUCH?" Greta wailed.

Mrs. Harper jumped up from the piano. She stared at me sternly with her hands at her waist.

Everyone in the auditorium was staring at me.

Becka and Greta screamed and cried, tugging the green skin on their cheeks.

"We know what you did to Reena!" Greta cried.

"We'll sue your family!" Becka shouted. "We'll have you arrested! The whole school will know you're a WITCH!"

"I — I —" I could only stammer. No words would come out.

My panic quickly turned to anger. This camera was ruining my life!

I swung it high — and smashed it against the back wall. Smashed it hard. Smashed it again. And again.

Gasping for air, my arms aching, I raised the camera to examine it.

It wasn't hurt at all. Not even a tiny dent.

I opened my mouth in a scream of rage. Pushed the door open and ran from the auditorium.

I was halfway to the front exit when my cell phone rang. I fumbled in my bag and pulled it out. "Mom!"

"Hi, Julie. I just wondered if —"

"Mom, I'm so glad you called!" I said in a trembling voice. "You've got to listen to me. I — I don't know what to do."

I leaned against the wall and pressed the phone to my ear. I told her the whole story. I started with Reena. Then I told her about Karla and her arm. I told her everything.

Mom listened without making a sound.

I ended by telling her what just happened to Becka and Greta, and how they blamed me and called me a witch.

"Wow," Mom muttered in a low voice. "Wow."

"What can I do, Mom?" I cried. "You've got to help me!"

"Julie," Mom said, "I know exactly what you need to do."

16

I gasped. "Huh? You *do*? Tell me!"

"Type it up, print it out, and give it to your creative writing teacher," Mom said. "It's an *excellent* story. Very clever. Really."

My mouth dropped open. "No, Mom. You got it wrong. Listen to me —"

"I like the supernatural part," Mom said. "Of course, your dad likes that sci-fi stuff more than me. But I've always said you have a great imagination. I think you take after your aunt Jenny. She —"

I gritted my teeth. I tried not to explode into a million pieces. "It's . . . not . . . a . . . story," I said slowly.

"What did you say?" Mom replied. "My phone is beeping. I'm getting another call. I'm still at work. Dinner may be a little late. Bye, dear."

She clicked off.

I heard voices. Three cheerleaders in their red-and-gold uniforms came skipping past me.

They practiced a cheer as they moved down the hall.

They seemed so happy. I slumped against the wall and watched them till they turned into the next hallway.

I never felt more frightened. I'd lost my best friend. I'd injured poor Karla, who was still in the hospital. And Becka and Greta were going to turn the whole school against me. Everyone would soon believe I was a witch.

A sob escaped my throat. I bit my lip. I didn't want to cry.

I shoved open the doors and ran outside. Into a cool, gray afternoon. A few raindrops were in the wind.

I didn't care about the weather. I didn't care about anything but getting rid of the evil camera.

I ran all the way home. I didn't stop at corners. I didn't look for oncoming cars. Houses and yards and streets passed me by in a gray blur. Like an out-of-focus photo.

I pulled open the front door and heard a cry.

"Julie!" Sammy ran up to greet me. His face was pale. His eyes were big and frightened.

"Help me!" he cried. "There's a *bee* in the house! It's going to *sting* me!"

Sammy was stung on the nose when he was three. He's been terrified of bees ever since.

He grabbed my hands and squeezed them. "Kill it! Kill it!"

"Sammy, are you home all by yourself?" I asked.

"Mrs. Kellins was here. But she had to run back to her house for a few minutes."

I heard a loud buzz. Sammy wasn't making it up. A fat yellow bumblebee swooped low over his head.

He screamed. "Kill it! Kill it!"

I swung my hand and tried to slap it away. The camera slipped out of my hand and hit the floor.

The bee soared high, then shot back, making a straight line for my face.

I swatted at it with both hands. It made an angry buzzing sound — and retreated to the window curtains.

I turned and saw Sammy pick up the camera.

"Nooooo —" I shouted. "Drop it! I mean it! Drop it!"

I saw the bee bounce off the front window. Then it came darting toward my little brother.

I swiped the camera out of Sammy's hands.

And it FLASHED.

17

Sammy grabbed the film as it slid out of the camera. He raised it close to his face to watch it develop.

"Give me that!" I cried. I grabbed for it. But he swung it out of my reach.

I had a sick feeling.

What have I done to my little brother?

The bee flew out the front window. That didn't make me feel any better.

"Awesome shot!" Sammy cried. He laughed. "Totally awesome shot of the bee!"

He handed the photo to me. My hand shook as I raised it to my face. It was a close-up of the bee. Sammy's face was completely hidden behind it.

"Weird," I muttered.

The bee looked gigantic. Like something out of a horror movie. And it appeared to be perched on Sammy's shoulders — in place of his head!

"Hey!" I cried out as another bright FLASH made me blink.

Oh, no . . .

As the explosion of color faded, I saw Sammy holding the camera. Another square of film came sliding out.

"Did — did you just take my picture?" I stammered.

He giggled. "It was my turn!"

"You idiot! You idiot!" I cried.

He laughed and danced around me. "What's your problem, Julie? Let's see how it came out."

He pressed next to me as we watched the picture develop.

"Totally awesome!" Sammy declared as it slowly came into focus.

At first, I thought I was holding it upside down. But I wasn't. The photo showed me *falling headfirst.*

Where was I?

I squinted hard at the picture. The background was a total blur. But I could see my face so clearly — screaming my head off as I fell.

Panic swept over me. "No! No! No!" I shouted.

I grabbed the photo — and ripped it to tiny shreds.

I tossed the shreds to the floor. I grabbed the camera away from my brother.

And then I opened my mouth in a shriek of horror.

"Sammy!"

His face — it was hidden. Hidden behind thick, yellow, spiky hair.

BEE hair!

Two skinny antennae poked up from the top of his furry head. They twitched back and forth. Sammy raised both hands and frantically tore at the wiry hair that covered his face.

"Sammy! Can you talk?" I screamed. "Can you see me? Can you *talk?*"

"BZZZZZZZZZZZZZZZ!"

The next morning, Mr. Webb called to congratulate me. He said I won the photo contest against David. I would be taking the big yearbook picture from the high diving board.

I barely replied. I think I muttered, "Thanks," and hung up.

I was too worried about Sammy. Mom and Dad had taken him to the hospital. He'd been there all night having tests.

Finally, Mom called. "What's up?" I cried. "How is Sammy?"

"The doctors are very puzzled," Mom said. Her voice was hoarse. She sounded very tired.

"They think maybe Sammy had an allergic reaction to something he ate," Mom said. "But Sammy keeps telling them a crazy story about a camera."

At least he stopped buzzing! I thought.

"Guess what?" Mom said. "Those two girls from your class — Becka and Greta? They're being examined in the next room. Some kind of skin problem. Just like in that story you told me. Isn't that weird?"

I sank to my knees on the floor. I realized I was pressing the phone so hard to my ear, I was giving myself a headache.

I took a long, deep breath. But it didn't help.

"I'll call you when we learn more," Mom said. She clicked off.

Of course I knew what Sammy's problem was. Becka and Greta, too. It was the evil camera.

But who would believe me? Mom still thought it was a story I made up!

I crossed my fingers and prayed the doctors would find a way to help Sammy, Becka, and Greta.

The camera was hidden deep in my closet. I'd been awake all night thinking about it.

At about three in the morning, I came up with a plan. A desperate plan to destroy the camera. And to reverse all the evil it had done. And to try to save my own life.

It was a crazy hope. But it was the only plan I could think up.

I glanced at the clock over the mantel. Time to go to school and shoot the big yearbook photo.

"You're a winner, Julie," I murmured to myself. I rolled my eyes bitterly. "Yeah. For sure. Big winner."

I pictured the photo Sammy had flashed of me.

I could see myself, falling ... falling head-first ... screaming in terror as I fell.

I hugged myself to stop shivering.

Was that photo about to come true? Would I be falling just like that off the high diving board?

Or would my plan save my life?

19

It was a glowing, sunny day. Not a cloud in the clear blue sky. A soft wind fluttered the flag in front of my school and made the trees whisper.

I made my way around to the new pool next to the soccer field. The building was long and low and white. The sun sparkled like gold in the wide glass doors.

A blast of warm air greeted me as I pulled open a door. Loud voices and laughter echoed off the white tile walls.

Teachers were already herding their classes into the empty swimming pool. Kids were laughing and goofing on each other — having fun.

I sighed. I knew today wasn't a fun day for me. I gazed up at the high diving board. A chill ran down my back.

A metal ladder stretched to the blue platform at the top. The rungs were narrow and steep. The platform looked a lot higher than I remembered.

I pictured myself falling headfirst from the diving board. I'd pictured it a thousand times during the night. But now it seemed a lot more real.

I stood there frozen, two cameras strapped around my neck. Kids' voices rang out from the pool. . . .

"Everybody start swimming!"

"Is this a race?"

"Hey, Tanya, did you wear it? Did you wear your string bikini?"

"Don't we need a lifeguard?"

I let out a cry as someone grabbed my hand. "Mr. Webb! Hi!"

"Everyone is ready for you, Julie," he said. "I just want to say congratulations again on winning the contest. I know you're going to do an excellent job up there."

We both raised our eyes to the high board.

If he only knew he is sending me up there to my doom.

Mr. Webb smiled at me and motioned me to the ladder. Then he flashed me a thumbs-up. "Break a leg!"

Oh, wow. Break a leg? I could break every bone in my body!

I turned and walked quickly to the ladder. Some kids in my class shouted to me from the pool.

"Julie, are you going to dive?"

"I'll catch you!"

"Take my picture now! In case you don't make it to the top!"

Ha-ha.

David stepped out from behind the ladder. He had three cameras strapped around his neck.

He stared at me hard. His face was tight with worry.

"Julie, are you *sure* you want me to do this?" he asked.

I nodded. "I told you last night, David. I just discovered I'm totally *terrified* of heights."

"But . . . you worked so hard to win our contest," he said.

"No biggie," I said. I gave him a little push toward the ladder. "Go. Do it. Take the picture, David. Have fun."

I stepped back and watched. David grabbed the railing and began to climb the ladder.

20

The kids in the pool pointed and shouted as David started his climb. His shoes clanged on the metal rungs of the ladder. Each thud rang in my ears.

Mr. Webb came running over to me. He grabbed my shoulder. "Julie, what's going on?" he demanded. "Why is David doing this instead of you?"

I sighed. "It's a very long story, Mr. Webb."

Mr. Webb wanted to ask me more questions. But I turned to watch David. He was halfway to the top, climbing slowly and steadily.

David will be safe up there, I told myself. *The evil camera didn't take a picture of him falling. So he won't fall.*

By staying down on the ground, I hoped I was breaking the camera's spell.

That was my big plan.

If I didn't go up on the diving board, the photo of me falling could not happen. I was defeating the camera's magic. Keeping its prediction from coming true.

Kids in the pool grew quiet as David stepped out onto the platform. He leaned against the railing and raised one of his cameras.

"People! Listen to me, people!" Mr. Webb shouted. "Raise your eyes to David and smile. Don't move. He's up high enough to get you all in."

I gazed up at David from the bottom of the ladder. High above me, he steadied himself against the metal rail.

Mr. Webb cupped his hands around his mouth and shouted to David. "At the count of three . . ."

He turned back to the kids in the pool. "Smile, everyone! Smile up at David. This is going to be *classic!*"

Typical. David is always David. He didn't wait for Mr. Webb to count to three. He stepped out onto the diving board. Then he raised his camera and started clicking away.

David dropped to his knees at the edge of the diving board to get closer to the kids. Then he leaned way forward to get the kids in the shallow end into the shot.

I realized I had stopped breathing.

He isn't going to fall, I told myself. *The picture shows ME falling — not David.*

I let my breath out slowly.

David changed cameras and clicked a dozen more shots.

Then the big showoff stood up on the edge of the diving board. "That's a wrap!" he shouted down to everyone. "Don't clap — just throw money!"

Kids laughed and groaned and shouted stuff back at him.

And then — typical David again. He decided to salute the crowd and take a deep bow.

I shut my eyes. I couldn't look.

Was he falling?

No.

When I opened my eyes, he was starting toward the ladder. He saw me and smiled. He gave me a quick wave.

Then he made a quick spin to take one more look at the crowd below. And that's when he lost his balance.

"He's FALLING!" I screamed.

Kids and teachers shrieked in horror. I saw some kids drop to their knees and cover their eyes. The screams were deafening.

As he started to drop, David reached out and grabbed the side of the diving board with both hands.

Yes! He managed to hold on.

I couldn't breathe, couldn't move a muscle. Just stared up at him, hands pressed against my cheeks, watching him dangle from the side of the board.

How long could he hold on?

"Help is on the way!" a teacher with a cell phone shouted. "Hang on! Help is on the way!"

I realized I had no choice. I stood at the bottom of the ladder. I took a deep breath and grabbed the railings.

My legs felt weak and trembly. I ignored them and pulled myself up.

Rung after rung.

"I'm coming!" I cried. "David — hold on!"

I didn't know if he could hear me over the screams of the kids and teachers below.

I pulled myself up another rung. . . . Another . . .

I reached the platform. I could see David's fingers gripping the sides of the diving board.

I dropped to my hands and knees. "Hold on, David!"

My heart pounded so hard, my chest ached. Crawling, I forced myself out onto the diving board.

I leaned over the side and grabbed David's wrists. I gripped them tightly. "I've *got* you!" I cried. "Swing your legs up. I'm holding you. Swing your legs onto the diving board."

David swung his body hard. One foot bumped the board — then dropped back down.

I felt a hard jolt but kept ahold of his wrists.

He tried again. This time, one leg sprawled over the board.

I gave a hard tug. *Yes!* Now he had one leg safely on the board. "Almost there, David. Almost . . ."

One more tug. Yes! I did it. I pulled him onto the edge of the board.

One more and he'd be safe. One more . . . I gave another pull, yanking him with all my strength.

I pulled so hard, I lost my balance.

"NOOOOOO!" A shrill scream escaped my throat as I felt myself start to fall.

And the thought flew through my mind: *The camera has WON!*

22

No!

On his stomach on the diving board, David swung his hands out — and grabbed me. Grabbed me before I could fall.

My knees banged the board. I fell facedown onto it. Pain shot up my body. But I was safe.

We both were safe.

We held on to each other, panting hard. Then we carefully stood up and started toward the ladder.

David grinned at me. "Julie, maybe we should be a *team*!"

"Yeah. Maybe," I agreed.

I heard the cheers of the kids down below. They were on their feet, staring up at David and me. They screamed and whistled and clapped happily.

I lowered myself slowly to the ground. I saw Mr. Webb and several other teachers running toward me.

But I didn't want to talk to anyone.

I just wanted to know one thing: *Did I defeat the evil camera?*

I ran home. Up to my room. I felt crazy. Dizzy. As if I were floating two feet off the ground. My whole body tingled.

I left the photos from the camera spread out on my desk. I lurched across the room and grabbed them.

Reena's picture was on top. I raised it close and squinted hard at it.

No red-eye. The red glow had disappeared from the photo.

Karla's picture had changed, too. It showed her jumping off the floor to shoot a layup.

"Yes!" I cried, pumping a fist in the air. "Yes!"

I dropped her photo and gazed at the one with Becka and Greta. Their skin was normal — not green! And in the last photo, my brother, Sammy, had his normal face. No yellow, spiky bee hair covering his face!

I did a little dance around my room. I pumped my fists in the air some more.

Had I *really* defeated the camera?

I grabbed my cell phone and dialed Mom at the hospital. "How is Sammy?" I asked.

I knew what Mom would say: "Sammy is fine. All that weird yellow hair suddenly fell out.

Becka and Greta are back to normal, too. Your dad and I are bringing Sammy home."

I knew it. I *knew* it!

The photo showed me falling headfirst to my death. But I kept it from coming true. And that broke the camera's magic.

And because I broke its magic, every horrible thing the camera did was reversed.

Now I had one more job. Now I had to destroy the camera so that no one else would ever find it and use it.

I thought I knew just how to do it.

I cleared all the junk off my dresser and tossed it onto the bed. Then I carefully dug the camera out from its hiding place in my closet.

This was my idea. . . .

The camera did terrible things to everyone it photographed. So all I had to do was make the camera take a picture of *itself*. And it would *do something terrible to ITSELF*!

Simple, right?

I knew it would work.

I set the camera down on my dresser top. And I pointed the lens at the mirror.

I checked the viewfinder. Perfect. The camera was set to take a perfect picture of itself in the mirror.

Now I had to make sure I didn't get in the snapshot.

I took a metal coat hanger from my closet. I stretched it out until it was almost a straight line.

Then I stood way to the side. I leaned way back. *No way* my reflection was going to show in the mirror.

Slowly . . . carefully . . . I stretched the hanger toward the camera.

And I lowered the end of the hanger . . . lowered it . . . until it pushed down on the shutter button.

FLASH!

Yes! The camera snapped a photo of itself in the mirror.

Would my plan work?

Holding my breath, I grabbed the square of film from the slot. I held it close to my face and stared at it as it developed.

"Come on . . . come on . . ."

And then I gasped. "Huh?"

I stared at the picture. Was I seeing *double*?

I looked down — and screamed.

"Oh, nooooooo!"

I stared at TWO evil cameras on my dresser, side by side!

ENTER
HORRORLAND

THE STORY SO FAR . . .

Several kids received mysterious invitations to be Very Special Guests at HorrorLand Theme Park. They looked forward to a week of scary fun. But the scares quickly became TOO REAL when Slappy the evil dummy, Dr. Maniac, and other menacing villains from the kids' past started to appear.

Two Very Special Guests — Britney Crosby and Molly Molloy — disappeared in a café with a mirrored wall. The other kids have been trying desperately to find them. The park guides — called Horrors — have been no help at all.

Except for one Horror, named Byron. He warned the kids they were all in danger. He said he'd help them escape from HorrorLand.

Escape where?

The kids keep finding clues about another theme park, called Panic Park. They don't know how to find Panic Park. But they know that *mirrors* play a big part in the mystery.

Why are there no mirrors anywhere in HorrorLand?

To find answers, Michael Munroe leads them down to the secret forbidden tunnels under HorrorLand. They are caught — and chased by Horrors. To help their escape, they let a bunch of ugly monsters out of their cages.

Now Michael has also vanished. The others are desperate to find him — and find their way out of the real horrors of HorrorLand!

Julie continues the story . . .

1

My first day in HorrorLand, and I couldn't wait to start taking pictures. I brought three cameras with me. Including the awesome new digital camera my dad bought me after I won the photo contest against David Blank.

Poor Sammy. When the invitation came to be a Very Special Guest at HorrorLand, he was totally *psyched*. But Mom and Dad had him signed up for four weeks of day camp.

Of course, he begged and cried and whined and pleaded and threw a tantrum. But . . . there was no way he could come with me.

I was glad I didn't have to take the little pest along. I wanted to hang out with the other Very Special Guests. And I wanted to take a *ton* of scary photos.

I unpacked my suitcase. Then I hurried out of Stagger Inn and headed to Zombie Plaza. It was a bright, sunny day, kind of hot and sticky.

Crowds of people jammed the plaza. I saw a row of small shops. At one end stood a creepy-looking building that resembled a castle. A marquee over the entrance read: HAUNTED THEATER.

I walked past a long line of people in front of a purple-and-green ice cream cart. *No.* Not ice cream. Big letters on the front of the cart read: NOSE CONES.

A Horror in a long purple apron was handing out ice cream cones shaped like human noses. "Everyone — come pick your nose!" he shouted. "Pick your nose! It's yummy!"

I snapped a few shots of him. He was funny. He slapped a frozen nose onto his nose and posed for me.

Across the plaza, I spotted a fortune-teller's booth. Behind the glass sat an old woman carved out of wood. She was dressed in a red velvet dress and had a turban on her head. MADAME DOOM.

I walked closer and raised my camera. I snapped a photo of the booth. But when I checked my picture out on the view screen, I had a surprise.

Standing next to the booth was a ventriloquist's dummy. He had big eyes, bright red lips, and an evil smile. He appeared to be standing up all on his own.

"Weird," I muttered. I turned back to Madame Doom's booth. No dummy standing there.

I flashed another picture.

The grinning dummy was there again! In this photo, he had one hand raised, *as if he was waving to me*!

But how could that be? Why couldn't I see him standing there?

I started over to the booth. But a loud *clang* made me stop. Startled, I nearly dropped my camera.

I spun around and saw a large grate in the middle of the walkway. The grate flew open, and a bald head popped up from underground.

At first, I thought it was a man. He had bright blue eyes. Human eyes.

But then I saw the pointed pig ears on top of his head, standing straight up.

And as he hoisted himself up through the grate opening, I gasped. His body was fat and covered with dark fur — like a gorilla.

What was a human head doing on that animal body?

He pulled himself onto the walkway. Then he turned and helped tug another creature out of the hole. The second creature looked just like him!

They both had big padded claws with curled talons, like bear paws.

They gnashed their teeth and growled. Thick yellow drool spilled from their mouths and plopped on the pavement.

Some people screamed and ran away. I saw two little girls start to cry. Their parents picked them up and hurried off with them.

Other people stared at the ugly creatures and laughed.

It had to be a HorrorLand joke — right?

I raised my camera. I snapped a few shots.

I stopped when I realized the two creatures had their bright blue eyes locked on me. They grunted to each other. Raised their talons . . .

. . . and came running at me, roaring like angry beasts.

I froze.

I dropped the camera, and it dangled at my waist from its strap.

Before I could move, I heard angry shouts: "Back! Get BACK!"

Four Horrors ran between me and the monsters. The Horrors carried long pointed sticks.

"Back!" they yelled. "Back! Get back!"

They jabbed the sticks at the two furry creatures.

The creatures snarled in rage. They swiped at the sticks with their big bear paws.

One creature grabbed a stick out of a Horror's hand — and hurled it into the crowd.

More people screamed and ran.

I raised my camera and snapped a few more shots. "This *has* to be some kind of show," I told myself. "The monsters are fake."

But why did the Horrors appear so frightened? Were they just good actors?

The groans and roars of the monsters rang out over the screams of the crowd. The Horrors jabbed the pointed sticks into the creatures' bellies.

"Back! Get back — NOW!"

"DOWN! Get back down there!"

I snapped picture after picture.

One of the monsters grabbed his belly and moaned. He backed into the open grate and disappeared down the hole. It took another few minutes to push and poke the other creature back down where he came from.

The Horrors rushed to slam the grate shut.

Two more Horrors came running over. They both seemed very alarmed.

"The monsters are still loose down there!" one of them cried. "We can't get them back in their cages."

"Those stupid kids who set them free — let's *find* them!" his partner shouted.

If this is all a show to scare people, I thought, *they're doing a really good job.*

I started to walk away. But I suddenly realized that all six Horrors were watching me.

Before I could move, they came running. They formed a circle around me. Two of the Horrors raised their pointed sticks.

A tall Horror with bright green fur and yellow eyes stretched out his hand. "Give me your camera," he growled.

I laughed. "You're joking — right?"

His yellow eyes darkened. "It's not a joke," he said. "Give me your camera — now!"

3

"You're not funny," I said. "You can't take my camera."

I tried to stuff it into my backpack.

But the Horror grabbed the camera out of my hand.

"Ow!" I screamed as the strap snapped and whipped my arm.

The Horror fumbled with the camera to open it. He tore out the memory card and tossed it as far as he could. Then he handed the camera back to me.

"Have a nice day," he said.

He and the others walked away. I could hear them muttering to each other about the escaped monsters.

I closed the camera and stuffed it into my backpack. My heart was pounding. I felt really upset.

They don't have the right to do that.

This is a free country!

Luckily, I had two other cameras in my pack and extra memory cards. I started to pull another camera out — when I saw a bunch of kids my age running across the plaza toward me.

They looked as if they'd been running a long way. They were red-faced, sweaty, and breathing hard.

A tall guy with dark hair hurried up to me. "Have you seen a big kid — very wide — kinda hulky — looks a little like a bulldog?" he asked.

"No," I said. "Is he lost or something?"

The other kids pulled up behind the tall boy. They all struggled to catch their breath.

"We can't find him," a girl said. "We're really freaked."

"Did you see the monsters?" a boy asked me.

"Yeah. They're totally lifelike," I said.

"They're not fake," the boy said. "They're real."

I rolled my eyes. "Real monsters?" I said. "Tell me another one."

"We're not kidding," a girl insisted. She told me her name was Abby. "Are you a Very Special Guest, too?"

I nodded. I told them my name. "I just arrived," I said. "I was looking for you guys."

The other kids introduced themselves quickly. There were seven of them. But I'm pretty good at remembering names.

I tried to memorize each one. There was Billy... Sheena... Matt... Carly Beth... Sabrina... Robby... and Abby.

Abby grabbed my arm. "You're lucky we found you," she said.

I frowned at her. "Why? What's up?"

Abby didn't let go of my arm. "We've got to get out of this park," she said. "Two girls have disappeared. And now Michael Munroe, too."

The tall boy named Matt glanced behind him. Then he turned back to me. "If you're one of us, you — you're in danger, Julie."

These kids were serious. It wasn't a joke.

"What kind of danger?" I asked. "This place is supposed to be good, scary fun, isn't it?"

Before they could answer, Carly Beth pointed across the plaza. "Guess who?" she said. "Here come the Monster Police!"

I turned and saw two tall Horrors in black-and-orange uniforms with shiny silver badges on their chests. They were trotting in our direction.

The kids took off, running toward the Haunted Theater. Abby glanced back. Saw me standing there, confused. She waved frantically for me to follow.

They were already far ahead of me. I started to run fast to catch up to them.

Why were they so afraid of the Monster Police?

I had a million questions I wanted to ask. But for now, I just wanted to make sure I didn't lose them as they dodged and darted through the crowds in the plaza.

They made a sharp turn. Ran between a couple of food carts. Then shot into a narrow, dark opening in a concrete wall.

I leaped over a baby stroller, my backpack bouncing on my shoulders. Abby was the last one to disappear into the opening.

The sign above it read: TUNNEL OF SCREAMS.

I hesitated for a moment. Then, breathing hard, I followed them into the tunnel.

I found myself in a narrow, black passageway. The light was so dim, I could only see shadows.

No way to tell how long the tunnel was. I could barely see two feet in front of me.

I heard voices. And the scrape of shoes on the floor.

I lurched forward, keeping one hand on the tunnel wall.

"Oh!" I gasped as I heard a girl's shrill scream.

I stopped. Pressed my hand on the wall.

Another scream. And then two boys shrieking, high and shrill.

I covered my ears. The screams seemed to be coming from everywhere — ahead of me . . . behind me . . . above me. . . .

"Hey — Abby!" I shouted. My voice echoed in the long tunnel. "Are you here? Carly Beth? Matt?"

No answer.

"AAAAAAAAGH!" A long, loud scream just ahead made me cover my ears. More shrieks and screams rang out, blaring louder... LOUDER.

I started to move again. Walking quickly now. I was desperate to get out of this creepy, dark tunnel. How long could it be?

The horrifying shrieks grew deafening. Painful. My ears throbbed. I could feel my heart racing in my chest.

The tunnel curved. Dim yellow light washed over me. I could see the shadows of people up ahead.

The deafening screams followed me.

And then I felt something sticky on my forehead. I pulled it off — a long, wet worm. I felt another one drop onto my shoulder. With a gasp, I pulled one out of my hair.

I looked up. I could see the worms dropping from the tunnel ceiling. Hundreds of them.

I tore them off my neck, out of my hair. A worm dropped into my mouth. I spit it out, gagging and choking.

The kids weren't lying, I thought. *There's something wrong with this park. Everything is too SCARY and too REAL to be fun!*

I started to run through the dim light, my shoes slapping the concrete tunnel floor. I slipped and slid on a thick puddle of worms on the floor.

Slapping at the worms with both hands, tearing them off my shoulders, my hair, I ran. Ran blindly through the long tunnel, the screams throbbing in my ears.

And then . . . a shrill scream over my head made me stop. Made me stop and gasp in horror. Because I recognized the voice.

It was MY SCREAM!

Panic shook my entire body. My breath caught in my throat.

Frozen in the darkness, I listened to my scream.

And then I remembered. The Horror in the entrance booth recorded me screaming when I first arrived at the park. He said it was so they could identify me later.

So . . . it's a joke after all. This is all a HorrorLand joke, I decided.

My legs were still trembling, but I started to walk again. A few seconds later, I saw bright daylight. The end of the tunnel!

"YAAAAAY!" I cheered as I stumbled out of the tunnel.

I blinked several times, waiting for my eyes to adjust to the bright light. I brushed a few more worms off my shoulders.

I shielded my eyes with one hand and searched for the other kids.

No sign of them.

Maybe they went back to the hotel, I decided. I was totally eager to catch up with them and find out what was really going on.

Why did they seem so scared?

Why did they think we Very Special Guests were in danger?

I took a few steps toward Stagger Inn — when a hand grasped my shoulder.

I let out a startled cry.

I turned to see a fierce-looking Horror. His shiny purple cape fluttered in the wind. He had short yellow horns curling up from his purple furry head.

I glimpsed the brass name tag on his chest. It read: BYRON.

"Let go of me!" I shouted.

But he squeezed my arm tighter. And jerked me off my feet.

He glanced all around. "Hurry!" he whispered. "I don't want them to see."

He started to pull me into the tunnel.

"Let go! What are you doing?" I screamed. "Why are you taking me back in there?"

5

"Let go of me!" I tried to swing out of his grasp. But he was too strong.

He pulled me into the darkness of the tunnel. I could hear the shrill screams echoing behind me. I felt like screaming, too!

"Don't be afraid," Byron whispered. "I came to help you."

"H-help me?" I stammered.

He let go of me. Then he shoved something into my hand.

"You can use this to escape," he said.

I blinked. "Escape? Escape from *what*?"

Byron's eyes darted to the tunnel entrance. He really did seem afraid of being caught.

"You've all got to get out of HorrorLand," he said. "You're not safe here."

"That's what those kids said," I told him. "But I don't understand —"

He raised a big hand to cut me off. "They

brought you here for a reason," he said. "You've got to get to the other park."

"Huh?" I squinted at him. "Other park? But I just got to *this* park!"

He shook his head. "Listen to me, Julie. You'll all be safe at the other park. Tell the others. Tell them I will try to help."

"I — I don't understand what you're talking about," I replied. "Why?"

He was staring past me, out into the light. I turned and saw two Horrors running toward us.

"You must hurry," Byron said. "The ones who brought you here are getting impatient!"

"But — but —" I sputtered.

"If they bring you to The Keeper," Byron said, "you are DOOMED!"

Then he took off, running hard.

The two Horrors spotted him. They began waving their arms and shouting for him to stop.

But Byron ducked and dodged his way through the crowd. After a short while, the two Horrors stopped and gave up the chase.

I stepped out of the tunnel. I began to follow the path that led to the hotel.

My head was spinning. I suddenly felt I was living in one of those underwater photos where everything is just a blue blur.

Byron's words kept repeating in my mind. But they didn't make any sense at all.

The other park? The Keeper?

Was he putting on a show? Like those monsters that climbed out from underground?

Was he *serious*?

I suddenly realized I had something gripped tightly in my hand. The thing Byron had given me in the tunnel.

I took a deep breath, trying to shake off my confusion. Then I raised my hand to examine whatever it was.

A piece of paper. It looked like an ad or something. It was wrapped around a small, hard object.

After I unwrapped it, I put the paper in my pocket and looked at what was left in my hand. A small hand mirror.

It was oval-shaped and had a short, red plastic handle.

What's the big deal about a mirror? I wondered. *Why did he give me this?*

Then I raised the mirror to my face — and let out a gasp.

"I look so AWFUL!" I cried.

I raised the mirror closer. My hair was a tangled mess. I brushed it out of my eyes. Then I pulled two more worms out of it.

My cheeks were pink and splotchy. I had a long dirt streak on my forehead.

From the tunnel?

I look as scary as a Horror! I thought. *Give me a cape and horns, and I can go to work in the park!*

Suddenly, I felt a strong pull. My head was being pulled toward the mirror. As if it were some kind of powerful magnet.

Before I realized it, my face was almost pressed against the glass. Was it some kind of trick mirror?

I didn't like it. It was creeping me out. I tossed the mirror into a tall metal trash can. Then I headed toward my room to freshen up.

"Julie? Hey — Julic!"

I stopped when I heard a girl calling my name. I turned and saw Abby waving to me frantically.

She and the other kids were huddled in a small grassy area at the side of the Haunted Theater. Matt and Carly Beth were perched on a park bench. The others were sitting on the grass in front of them.

They had all been talking at once. But they stopped when I came trotting over.

"Where were you?" Carly Beth asked.

"I lost you in that screaming tunnel," I said. I sighed. "That was a creepy place."

"It gets a lot creepier than that," Robby said.

"Well . . . you won't believe what happened to me," I said. "A big Horror pulled me back into the tunnel and started giving me all kinds of warnings."

Matt leaned forward on the bench. They all raised their eyes to me.

"Warnings? Tell us what he said," Matt said.

I stepped up beside his bench so I could face everyone. "His name is Byron," I said. "I read his name tag and —"

"You saw Byron?" Carly Beth cried. "Where?"

They all seemed to get very tense.

"I told you," I said. "He pulled me into the tunnel. Do you know him?"

"Go on," Matt said. "Tell us everything he said."

"He warned me that we were all in danger," I said. "He said we have to get to the other park. And he . . . he gave me this."

I pulled the piece of paper out of my pocket.

Matt and Carly Beth jumped up from their seats. The others gathered around me.

"Let's see it," Robby said.

I unfolded it and held it up to them. It looked like an old ad. The color picture at the top showed some kind of café or ice cream place.

The tables all had blue-and-white-checked tablecloths. I saw mirrors on all the walls.

These old-fashioned-looking kids sat at the tables. They were all eating huge ice cream sundaes from tall glass dishes.

Beneath the picture in big, bold type, it read: STUBBY'S SUNDAE SHACK. 10 Panic Park Drive.

"I don't *believe* it!" Matt cried.

"This is totally incredible!" the girl named Sheena exclaimed.

The kids all started talking at once. They passed the page around and kept staring at it, saying how awesome and amazing it was.

"I don't get it," I said. "What's the big deal?"

They didn't hear me.

So I shouted. "I don't understand! Please explain this to me!"

"The two girls who disappeared," Billy said. "That's where they disappeared." He jabbed his finger at the page.

"In that café?" I asked.

"We were there," Billy's sister, Sheena, said breathlessly. "We saw Britney and Molly through the window. But when we went inside . . ."

". . . they were gone." Billy finished her sentence for her.

"We were in that café," Matt said. "We were right there. But it isn't in HorrorLand. See the address? Stubby's Sundae Shack is in Panic Park. The other park."

I shook my head hard. "This isn't making sense," I said. "Are you saying that you were in *two parks* at once?"

"No. We were in our hotel. In Stagger Inn," Sheena said. "But the café appeared . . ."

"It just appeared from out of nowhere," Billy said.

"I put my hand in that mirror," Sheena said, pointing to the picture. "And it went right in. The mirror was soft. And . . ."

"Sheena went invisible for a while," Matt told me. "Then she disappeared, too. Just like Britney and Molly."

"I think I went into the café mirror or something," Sheena said. "I went to the other park."

"Through the mirror?" I asked.

"Mirrors are important," Matt said. "Mirrors are an important clue. We think maybe that's how we can get to the other park."

I slapped my forehead. "I don't BELIEVE it!" I cried. "Byron . . . that Horror Byron. He gave me a mirror!"

"He WHAT?" Matt said.

"He gave me a hand mirror," I said. "He told me to use it. But . . . but I didn't understand."

"He was trying to help us escape this place," Carly Beth said. "Julie, we've been searching *everywhere* for a mirror!"

"This is *awesome* news!" Billy declared.

"What did you do with it?" Sabrina demanded. "Is it in your backpack?"

"Give it to us!" Robby cried.

"That mirror is our way out of here!" Matt said. He pumped his fists in the air. "Yes! Yessss!"

They turned to me. I suddenly felt sick. I could feel the blood rush to my face. I knew I was blushing.

"I . . . I . . ." I started. I couldn't get the words out.

Finally, I confessed. "I tossed it away. I didn't know . . ."

They groaned and sighed and shook their heads. I felt so bad.

Abby grabbed my hand. "Where did you throw

it away, Julie? Do you remember where you tossed it?"

"I . . . think so," I said. "It was a tall metal trash can. I think it was right outside the exit to the Tunnel of Screams."

"Show us," Matt said.

I turned and took off running. They all followed close behind.

No one said a word. I kept praying the mirror would still be there. I just met these kids, and I'd already let them down.

We passed a food cart selling ROADKILL WAFFLES. I didn't slow down to see what they were.

A Horror was passing out free plastic fangs to kids. He kept shouting, "Fang you very much! Fangs a lot! Fang you kindly!"

The park seemed normal and fun. But I'd been here for less than a day, and I already knew that it wasn't. Something was wrong in HorrorLand. I believed I was in danger. Real danger.

Running hard, I saw the black tunnel exit up ahead. A few feet away stood the trash can.

And then I stopped — and uttered a horrified cry: "NOOOOO!"

A bright purple garbage truck was parked a few feet from the trash can. I could hear it roar as it chewed up trash.

A Horror in a long purple apron picked up the

trash can in his purple gloves. He was carrying the can to the truck to empty it.

"No — please!" I tried to scream. But my voice choked in my throat. "Please —"

"No! Wait!" Matt shouted to the Horror. "Wait! Please! Don't dump that can! Please WAIT!"

I gasped as the Horror hoisted up the trash can. He tilted it to the back of the truck — and dumped everything in.

With a low roar, the truck instantly began to grind up the trash.

We ran up to the Horror as he set the empty can back on the ground. He turned to us and raised a gloved hand to one of his horns.

"Sorry," he shouted. "What did you kids say? I couldn't hear you over the noise of the truck."

"Never mind." Carly Beth groaned, shaking her head.

I let out a sigh. I looked around at the unhappy faces.

These kids must think I'm a total jerk, I told myself. *That Horror Byron gave me something important, and I just tossed it in the trash.*

The Horror climbed behind the wheel, and the truck rumbled away. We stood there watching it go.

"*Now* what do we do?" Sheena asked. "We were *so close.*"

"I . . . I'm sorry," I muttered.

"We can't stand here feeling sorry for ourselves," Abby said.

"Abby is right," Carly Beth agreed. "There are eight of us, right? We should be able to think of something. Let's get out of here — right now."

"But how?" Billy asked. "We can't just walk out the front exit."

Matt's dark eyes flashed. A smile crossed his face. "Why *can't* we?" he cried. "Hey — why *can't* we walk out the front exit? That's totally *brilliant!*"

He slapped Billy on the back.

Billy frowned at him. "You're joking, right?"

"I'm not joking," Matt said. "We just walk out the front gate the way we came in. No problem."

"I don't think so," Carly Beth said. "The Horrors . . . they've tried very hard to keep us here."

"But three kids have *already* escaped HorrorLand!" Robby said. "Molly and Britney and Michael. They escaped to the other park — right?"

"We don't really know *where* those three kids are," Sabrina said. "Maybe they're in the other park. Maybe they're not."

I glanced across Zombie Plaza. Two MP's in their black-and-orange uniforms were leaning against the wall of a souvenir store called GUTS 'N' STUFF.

Were they watching us?

Carly Beth spotted them, too. I saw her shiver.

"Listen, guys," she said. "We're not going to feel safe until we're out of this park. So I think we should head to the front gate and check it out."

"She's right," Matt agreed. "We've got to give it a try. Maybe we can sneak out."

"For sure," Billy said. "We can think up a way to distract the guards. And then we can run through the exit and keep running."

"I'll bet our cell phones will work outside the park," Abby said. "We can call our parents. We can call for help."

Everyone started talking at once. Some kids didn't believe they'd even let us *get* to the front gate. But we all agreed it was worth a try.

We began walking quickly. Away from the plaza, along the side of our hotel, then along the curving path that led to the exit gate.

I kept glancing back to see if the MP's were following us. I didn't see them.

It was early afternoon. The exit gate wasn't crowded. Most people were staying till evening.

As we walked closer, I saw four exit turnstiles. A sign with a big arrow read: SURVIVORS — THIS WAY.

There were two small booths next to the turnstiles. One of them was empty. A Horror sat in the other one, reading a magazine.

My heart began to race. My hands were suddenly ice-cold. I knew the others were really tense, too.

"Come on. Keep walking, everyone," Carly Beth whispered.

We stepped past the Horror in his booth and approached the turnstiles.

"Eyes straight ahead," Carly Beth whispered. "Don't stop. Don't look back. Let's go. We're out of here!"

I held my breath. We all kept walking. Matt reached the turnstile first. He raised his hands to push his way out.

And behind us in the booth, the Horror shouted: "Hey, you kids — STOP RIGHT THERE!"

Caught.

Matt groaned and dropped back from the turn-stile. "I *knew* this was too easy," he muttered.

We turned as the Horror came hurrying over to us. He was huge and powerful-looking, with a big belly that bounced in front of him as he ran.

He had purple fur all over his body. Purple, spiky hair. Long, dark horns that stood straight up on his head. His eyes were red and angry.

"Wait right there!" he boomed. "Don't anybody move!"

So close, I thought. *We came so close.*

I could see the rows of cars in the big parking lot on the other side of the turnstiles.

The Horror bulled his way in front of us. He was using his big body to block us from the exit. His hands were balled into fists at his sides.

His name tag was covered up by his fur, so I couldn't read his name.

I took a step back. My heart raced even faster. This dude was *scary*!

"Are you leaving?" he boomed. His voice rumbled from his belly, like thunder.

"Do you think we allow people to escape from HorrorLand *alive*?" he demanded.

We stared at him in silence.

Then he laughed. "Just joking," he said. He slapped Billy on the back. "I think I really scared you! Ha!"

"I . . . I . . ." Billy couldn't get any words out.

The Horror pulled a small, square object from his uniform pocket. "If you are leaving," he said, "better let me stamp your hand. You know. In case you want to return."

Stamp our hands?

My mouth dropped open. The others were in shock, too.

We lined up. The Horror took a wooden stamp, rubbed it on his purple ink pad. Then he stamped a purple H on our right hands.

"Hope you had a HORRIFYING time!" he said.

Matt didn't hesitate. He pushed through the turnstile. On the other side, he started to trot to the parking lot.

Carly Beth followed him out. Sabrina was right behind her.

One by one, all eight of us pushed our way out through the turnstile.

I was the last one out of the park. As I stepped into the parking lot, I turned back to see if the Horror was watching us.

No. He had returned to his booth.

We kept close together as we made our way down an aisle of parked cars.

When we were out of sight of the exit booth, Billy leaped into the air. "Awesome!" he shouted. "Awesome!" He and his sister, Sheena, pumped their fists in the air, then touched knuckles.

We all burst out laughing. It was such a relief!

Carly Beth had a huge grin on her face. "I don't believe it!" she cried. "We're out! We *made* it! That was *so easy!*"

The hot sun beamed down on us. The rows and rows of cars gleamed in the sunlight.

Matt glanced all around. Then he turned back to us. "*Now* what?" he asked.

I fumbled in my backpack for my cell phone. I pulled it out and flipped it open.

I shook my head. I held the phone up so the others could see. "No service," I muttered.

Robby stared at his phone. "I don't have any bars, either. Guess we have to move farther away from the park," he said.

Matt slapped his hand on a car roof. "Where *is* everyone? Maybe we can get someone to give us a lift to the nearest town."

"Good idea," I said. "Then we can — oh!" I let out a sharp cry. I felt kind of weird. Kind of fluttery.

My right hand started to itch really bad. I started to scratch it. That didn't help.

I squinted at the back of my hand. "Oh, *no*!" I screamed. "Look!"

I held my hand up. "The purple H that Horror stamped! It's GROWING!" I cried.

I stared in shock. I couldn't believe it!

The lines of the H were growing longer, spreading over the back of my hand.

"Oh, wow! Mine, too!" Sabrina gasped.

"Mine, too!"

"Ohhhhh, it itches! It really itches!"

In seconds, we all began scratching the backs of our hands. Staring in horror as the purple lines grew longer.

And then . . . and then . . . the lines began to sprout. Like slender purple weeds.

They popped off the skin and stretched right off our hands.

I grabbed at mine. I wrapped my fingers around the growing, stretching strings — and gave a hard tug to pull them off.

"OUCH!" I screamed. They were *attached* to my hand. Stuck into my skin.

Like jungle vines, they reached up, growing faster. Growing *fatter*.

"It's like SNAKES!" I cried. "It's like snakes growing right out of my hand!"

The purple tendrils twisted in the air, rising higher. Like they were reaching up toward the sun.

"Help! Oh, help!"

"I can't pull it off! OUCH!"

I tried snapping my hand back and forth. I tried tugging at the tendrils again.

But they were as strong as electrical cords — and stretching fast.

124

We were all screaming and thrashing our hands around, trying to fight the growing vines. But there was no way to stop them.

They grew so fast! The tendrils snaking from my hand were at least six feet long now!

They stood up high. Then lowered themselves quickly. And began to wrap around me. They wrapped around and around me — tightening like elastic.

Tightening . . . tightening . . .

"HELP!"

"SOMEBODY!"

We were all screaming now. Trying to squirm out from under the thick vines growing from our own hands.

They wrapped around my body . . . climbed higher . . . stretched around my head now. So hard to see.

I realized the vines were tying us together . . . all eight of us . . . trapped inside their tight net.

Holding us . . . holding us down . . .

Couldn't move. So hard to breathe. Tightening . . . tightening around us . . .

Is someone going to help us?

Are we going to suffocate out here?

Is this . . . the END?

To be continued in . . .

Goosebumps HorrorLand™

#9 WELCOME TO CAMP SLITHER

But first . . .

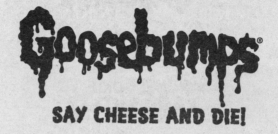

Greg toppled backward onto the ground. *"Aah!"* he screamed. Then he realized the others were laughing.

"It's that dumb cocker spaniel!" Shari cried. "He followed us!"

"Go home, dog. Go home!" Bird shooed the dog away.

The dog trotted to the curb, turned around, and stared back at them, its stubby tail wagging furiously.

Feeling embarrassed that he'd become so frightened, Greg slowly pulled himself to his feet, expecting his friends to give him grief. But they were staring up at the Coffman house thoughtfully.

"Yeah, Michael's right," Bird said, slapping Michael hard on the back, so hard Michael winced and turned to slug Bird. "Lets see what it's like in there."

"No way," Greg said, hanging back. "I mean, the place is kind of creepy, don't you think?"

"So?" Shari challenged him, joining Michael and Bird, who repeated her question: "So?"

"So . . . I don't know," Greg replied. He didn't like being the sensible one of the group. Everyone always made fun of the sensible one. He'd rather be the wild and crazy one. But somehow he always ended up sensible.

"I don't think we should go in there," he said, staring up at the neglected old house.

"Are you chicken?" Bird asked.

"Chicken!" Michael joined in.

Bird began to cluck loudly, tucking his hands into his armpits and flapping his arms. With his beady eyes and beaky nose, he looked just like a chicken.

Greg didn't want to laugh, but he couldn't help it.

Bird *always* made him laugh.

The clucking and flapping seemed to end the discussion. They were standing at the foot of the broken concrete steps that led up to the screened porch.

"Look. The window next to the front door is broken," Shari said. "We can just reach in and open the door."

"This is cool," Michael said enthusiastically.

"Are we really doing this?" Greg, being the

sensible one, had to ask. "I mean — what about Spidey?"

Spidey was a weird-looking man of fifty or sixty they'd all seen lurking about town. He dressed entirely in black and crept along on long, slender legs. He looked just like a black spider, so the kids all called him Spidey.

Most likely he was homeless or a drifter. No one really knew anything about him — where he'd come from, where he lived. But a lot of kids had seen him hanging around the Coffman house.

"Maybe Spidey doesn't like visitors," Greg warned.

But Shari was already reaching in through the broken windowpane to unlock the front door. And after little effort, she turned the brass knob and the heavy wooden door swung open.

One by one, they stepped into the front entryway, Greg reluctantly bringing up the rear. It was dark inside the house. Only narrow beams of sunlight managed to trickle down through the heavy trees in front, creating pale circles of light on the worn brown carpet at their feet.

The floorboards squeaked as Greg and his friends made their way past the living room, which was bare except for a couple of overturned grocery store cartons against one wall.

Spidey's furniture? Greg wondered.

The living room carpet, as threadbare as the one in the entryway, had a dark oval stain in the center of it. Greg and Bird, stopping in the doorway, both noticed it at the same time.

"Think it's blood?" Bird asked, his tiny eyes lighting up with excitement.

Greg felt a chill on the back of his neck. "Probably ketchup," he replied. Bird laughed and slapped him hard on the back.

Shari and Michael were exploring the kitchen. They were staring at the dust-covered counter as Greg and Bird stepped up behind them. They saw immediately what had captured their attention. Two fat, gray mice were standing on the counter, staring back at Shari and Michael.

"They're cute," Shari said. "They look just like cartoon mice."

The sound of her voice made the two rodents scamper along the counter, around the sink, and out of sight.

"They're gross," Michael said, making a disgusting face. "I think they were rats — not mice."

"Rats have long tails. Mice don't," Greg told him.

"They were definitely rats," Bird muttered, pushing past them and into the hallway. He disappeared toward the front of the house.

Shari reached up and pulled open a cabinet over the counter. Empty. "I guess Spidey never uses the kitchen," she said.

Well, I didn't *think* he was a gourmet chef," Greg joked.

He followed her into the long, narrow dining room, as bare and dusty as the other rooms. A low chandelier still hung from the ceiling, so brown with caked dust it was impossible to tell that it was glass.

"Looks like a haunted house," Greg said softly.

"*Boo*," Shari replied.

"There's not much to see in here," Greg complained, following her back to the dark hallway. "Unless you get a thrill from dustballs."

Suddenly, a loud *crack* made him jump.

Shari laughed and squeezed his shoulder.

"What was *that*?" he cried, unable to stifle his fear.

"Old houses *do* things like that," she said. "They make noises for no reason at all."

"I think we should leave," Greg insisted, embarrassed again that he'd acted so frightened. "I mean, it's boring in here."

"It's kind of exciting being somewhere we're not supposed to be," Shari said, peeking into a dark, empty room — probably a den or study at one time.

"I guess," Greg replied uncertainly.

They bumped into Michael. "Where's Bird?" Greg asked.

"I think he went down to the basement," Michael replied.

"Huh? The basement?"

Michael pointed to an open door at the right of the hallway. "The stairs are there."

The three of them made their way to the top of the stairs. They peered down into the darkness. "Bird?"

From somewhere deep in the basement, his voice floated up to them in a horrified scream: "Help! It's got me! Somebody — please help! It's *got* me!

"It's got me! It's got me!"

At the sound of Bird's terrified cries, Greg pushed past Shari and Michael, who stood frozen in openmouthed horror. Practically flying down the steep stairway, Greg called out to his friend. "I'm coming, Bird! What *is it*?"

His heart pounding, Greg stopped at the bottom of the stairs, every muscle tight with fear. His eyes searched frantically through the smoky light pouring in from the basement windows up near the ceiling.

"Bird?"

There he was, sitting comfortably, calmly, on an overturned metal trash can, his legs crossed, a broad smile on his birdlike face. "Gotcha," he said softly, and burst out laughing.

"What *is* it? What *happened*?" came the frightened voices of Shari and Michael. They clamored down the stairs, coming to a stop beside Greg.

It took them only a few seconds to scope out the situation.

"Another dumb joke?" Michael asked, his voice still trembling with fear.

"Bird — were you goofing on us again?" Shari asked, shaking her head.

Enjoying his moment, Bird nodded, with his peculiar half grin. "You guys are too easy," he scoffed.

"But, Doug —" Shari started. She only called him Doug when she was upset with him. "Haven't you ever heard of the boy who cried wolf? What if something bad happens sometime, and you really need help, and we think you're just goofing?

"What could happen?" Bird replied smugly. He stood up and gestured around the basement. "Look — it's brighter down here than upstairs."

He was right. Sunlight from the backyard cascaded down through four long windows at ground level, near the ceiling of the basement.

"I still think we should get out of here," Greg insisted, his eyes moving quickly around the large, cluttered room.

Behind Bird's overturned trash can stood an improvised table made out of a sheet of plywood resting on four paint cans. A nearly flat mattress, dirty and stained, rested against the wall, a faded wool blanket folded at the foot.

"Spidey must *live* down here!" Michael exclaimed.

Bird kicked his way through a pile of empty food boxes that had been tossed all over the floor — TV dinners, mostly. "Hey, a Hungry Man dinner!" he exclaimed. "Where does Spidey heat these up?"

"Maybe he eats them frozen," Shari suggested. "You know. Like Popsicles."

She made her way toward a towering oak wardrobe and pulled open the doors. "Wow! This is *excellent*!" she declared. "Look!" She pulled out a ratty-looking fur coat and wrapped it around her shoulders. "Excellent! she repeated, twirling in the old coat.

From across the room, Greg could see that the wardrobe was stuffed with old clothing. Michael and Bird hurried to join Shari and began pulling out strange-looking pairs of bell-bottom pants, yellowed dress shirts with pleats down the front, tie-dyed neckties that were about a foot wide, and bright-colored scarves and bandannas.

"Hey, guys —" Greg warned. "Don't you think maybe those belong to somebody?"

Bird spun around, a fuzzy red boa wrapped around his neck and shoulders. "Yeah. These are Spidey's dress-up clothes," he cracked.

Check out this *baad* hat," Shari said, turning around to show off the bright purple wide-brimmed hat she had pulled on.

"Neat," Michael said, examining a long blue cape. "This stuff must be at least twenty-five years old. It's awesome. How could someone just leave it here?"

"Maybe they're coming back for it," Greg suggested.

As his friends explored the contents of the wardrobe, Greg wandered to the other end of the large basement. A furnace occupied the far wall, its ducts covered in thick cobwebs. Partially hidden by the furnace ducts, Greg could see stairs, probably leading to an outside exit.

Wooden shelves lined the adjoining wall, cluttered with old paint cans, rags, newspapers, and rusty tools.

Whoever lived here must have been a real handyman, Greg thought, examining a wooden worktable in front of the shelves. A metal vise was clamped to the edge of the worktable. Greg turned the handle, expecting the jaws of the vise to open.

But to his surprise, as he turned the vise handle, a door just above the worktable popped open. Greg pulled the door all the way open, revealing a hidden cabinet shelf.

Resting on the shelf was a camera.

For a long moment, Greg just stared at the camera.

Something told him the camera was hidden away for a reason.

Something told him he shouldn't touch it. He should close the secret door and walk away.

But he couldn't resist it.

He reached onto the hidden shelf and took the camera in his hands.

It pulled out easily. Then, to Greg's surprise, the door instantly snapped shut with a loud *bang*.

Weird, he thought, turning the camera in his hands.

What a strange place to leave a camera. Why would someone put it here? If it were valuable enough to hide in a secret cabinet, why didn't he take it with him?

MEMO

To: All Crude Cart Staff
From: Mr. Pew K. Latte
Re: Crude Cart Guidelines

It has been brought to my attention that some Crude Cart workers are not adhering to HorrorLand FDA* Requirements.

Please review the following guidelines to keep your carts unclean, unsafe, and unhealthy:

- Accept delivery from Ripe Garb Age Service every morning.

- Kids will be demanding extra larvae and extra maggots. Keep a good supply.

- If you sneeze on the food you are selling, simply wipe it off on the front of your shirt.

If you have any questions, please direct them to yourself.

*Foul and Disgusting Administration

FIND THE REst at
WWW.ESCAPEHorrorLAND.COM
—LIZZY

THE
PLAY PEN

Scream Your Head off

PRIZES

ROAD
KILL
WAFFLES

MAP
8

Connects to Map #7

About the Author

R.L. Stine's books are read all over the world. So far, his books have sold more than 300 million copies, making him one of the most popular children's authors in history. Besides Goosebumps, R.L. Stine has written the teen series Fear Street and the funny series Rotten School, as well as the Mostly Ghostly series, The Nightmare Room series, and the two-book thriller *Dangerous Girls*. R.L. Stine lives in New York with his wife, Jane, and Minnie, his King Charles spaniel. You can learn more about him at www.RLStine.com.

COME FAMILIES! COME FRIENDS! TO A PLACE THAT'S GRAND! FOR FUN AND THRILLS, VISIT HORRORLAND!

WITH TWISTS AND TURNS AND FLIPS AND SPINS! OUR RIDES ARE A RIOT! SO STRAP YOURSELF IN!

IF YOUR TUMMY IS GRUMBLY, PLEASE DON'T BE SHY! WE'VE GOT OODLES OF TREATS TO TRY!

SO COME FOR ADVENTURE AND FANTASY TOO! YOUR HORRORLAND FRIENDS WILL BE WAITING FOR YOU!

Read the books. Play the games.
Defeat the Dummy.
www.EnterHorrorLand.com

NOW A MAJOR
MOTION PICTURE
JACK BLACK
Goosebumps
VILLAGE ROADSHOW PICTURES
THIS FILM IS NOT YET RATED.
FOR FUTURE INFO GO TO
FILMRATINGS.COM
/GoosebumpsTheMovie
SCHOLASTIC
COLUMBIA PICTURES
a Sony Company